Forbidden Horses

Book Three of the Forbidden Trilogy

Joanne Lewis

Soul Attitude Press

Forbidden Horses

Cover designed by Johnny Breeze

Published by Soul Attitude Press

Pinellas Park, FL

www.soulattitudepress.com

Visit the author website: http://www.joannelewiswrites.com

ISBN: 9781939181763 (eBook)

ISBN: 9781939181749 (Paperback)

First Edition

Forbidden Horses

Book Three of the Forbidden Trilogy

Prologue
Turkey 1171

Fatima Yannatou knelt next to the Amu Darya River. Her delicate hands labored to fill round clay containers with water. The Turkish sun stroked the twelve-year-old's tawny skin. A Caspian tiger watched lazily from across the river bank. In the distance, the big mountain textured the sky. Nimble and efficient, she added lavender leaves to the spheres and packed the openings of the containers with mud. Her long dark hair tangled with sand and sweat. She had worked ably since five years old and was pleased to have beaten the other children for this job. As payment, she'd be permitted to observe the *carosella* up close.

"There, that's number fifteen." She closed her eyes and inhaled the aromatic lavender. Another deep inhale, and she imagined herself to be worthy of fragrance sprayed upon her as she sat at a make-up table. She put her feet in the river, and pretended a Hebrew maid applied a concoction of purple and red berries to soothe her sunburned cheeks.

"Bring the cylinders here, servant girl." Dmitry yelled from the arena, a clay pot's throw away.

Startled by the intruder into her fantasy, she jumped, lifted two of the balls, and cradled them as if a babe in each arm. She waddled under their weight toward Dmitry. With each step, the arena seemed to lunge farther from her. Her shoulders and neck ached. Daily, she balanced pots of water on her head and walked distances four times as long without issue, but during those times she laughed with her sister and listened to fables shared by her mother and the time easily slipped past. Now, she sought motivation to keep moving—one bare foot in front of the other—by imagining the thrill she would feel at watching this grand event, so anticipated by all the villagers. Finally at the arena, her hair mopped to her face with sweat, she looked up at the horses that were tethered to posts. The broad chested steeds snorted and stamped as if aware the game was about to begin, or perhaps they smelled the tiger. Where there was one, there were more.

The sand that lined the arena was light as dust and scattered on the wings of the hot breeze. Slaves carted in silt to add to the grounds. The sand could be calmed, but not the wind.

As the rich and royal spectators arrived, Fatima endured seven more trips. Two green eyed tigers now watched the girl from the banks of the Amu. With the sacks lined up at the arena, Fatima rested her palms on her knees. The girl was breathless and drenched in sweat. Sand caked the oval points of her eyes, layered in her nostrils, and blanketed her tongue. Fatigue bedded in her bones, and then dissipated, launched away on the wind. The horsemen, as regal and gallant as their mounts, had arrived.

The game was *garosello*, translated as "little war" in Italian, and called *carosella* in Spanish. A military exercise invented by Turks as training for cavalrymen. The rules were simple: officers and members of the regiment galloped on horseback in a circular sand-filled ring and torpedoed clay balls of perfumed water at each other. Losers who were splashed with the fragrant water were not permitted to bathe in the river for two days. Immersed in the womanly smell, the cavalrymen were berated. Shame was brought to their families. Winners were celebrated like heroes who had returned from battle. After the two days of humiliation ended, the perfumed men washed. Criticism ceased. Among slaps on the back and hoisted boza, family reputations were restored. All in good fun.

Horses and riders entered the ring. Fatima stared, mesmerized. Eleven in all, she counted. A handsome uniformed man with a red sash across his shoulder and a sword looped through his belt sat atop a white Arabian with a bronze mane and tail. The horse galloped around the ring with short, powerful strides, the muscles of its broad chest lyrical. The beast strong and beautiful, like no other creature she had every witnessed.

The mass of spectators roared when a general tossed the first clay ball into the air. A barrel-chested officer who rode a palomino grabbed the ball and swiftly whipped the orb toward the rider atop the Arabian. Caught, the cavalryman flung it toward a soldier on a chocolate bay. The rider adroitly aimed for a swordsman on a spotted Appaloosa. The app shied at the sight of the fast-moving ball, which knocked his rider off balance. The clay missile hit the rider in the chest. Perfumed water exploded all over him, over his mount.

The crowd roared so loud Fatima looked to the sky for thunderous clouds but all was clear. She looked toward the big mountain but no fire spewed from its mouth. The tigers scattered. She laughed and raised her arms with glee. Head hung, the lavender-scented swordsman trotted his horse to the side and dismounted to the jeers of the other riders and the taunts of the spectators.

Fatima clapped and cheered. She had never had so much fun. She wished her sister was with her. As the game resumed, Fatima memorized each horse, their colors, the swing of their tails and manes, and the striations of their muscled haunches. She wished, more than anything, to mount one of the horses and ride round and round the circle of sand, positive with a single leap she and the horse could fly.

*

The twelfth-century Turkish training exercise of cavalrymen who tossed clay balls filled with perfumed water at rivals became a popular spectator sport. By the 1500s, French horsemen copied the tradition and morphed the game into an equestrian competition. Labeled *carrousel* by the French, the military equine drill suspended legless wooden horses on ropes from beams attached to poles. Men, horses, mules, or oxen rotated the poles, which caused the wooden horses to swing and bob. Holding lances, riders sat upon the prancing horses and attempted to snare a hanging steel ring.

Like Fatima, who centuries earlier had cheered when cavalrymen threw perfumed balls at each other, French bystanders enjoyed *carrousel* and wanted more. By the mid-1700s, the demand was met. Legless horses designed by the French for military exercises were turned into carousels for entertainment. The populace paid to ride the wooden horses that paraded in a circle. Imagining their mounts to be real, the riders attempted to snare a metal ring with a long stick. At the *Place du Carrousel* in Paris, adults and children rode wooden horses on one of the earliest versions. Like the military training tool, the horses were suspended from overhead wood beams and were rotated by man or horse.

Versions of the carousel appeared at fairs and festivals throughout Europe.

Crowds gathered. Queues often trailed off fairgrounds and snarled traffic. The early carousels were limited in size and speed, as they could only be moved as fast as a man or horse could rotate the pole.

On New Year's Day 1861, Thomas Bradshaw unveiled the first steam-powered carousel in England. The Golden Age of the Carousel began, ending like so many things with the Great Depression and the advent of World War II.

Chapter One

February 14, 1791

Her vision blurred, Countess Anna von Walsegg discerned strange movements in the dark. Her mouth was dry and her taste buds deadened. Her breath reeked of hereafter. Her husband, Count Franz von Walsegg, a wealthy landowner whose family made their fortune in gypsum mining, whimpered at her bedside. His tears fell from his bottom lids and landed on Anna's cheeks, pricking her skin like daggers. Alcohol fumes swarmed from his breath and pores.

"Stand aside." Father Mattheus Richter elbowed his way toward Anna's bed.

The pudgy, frocked priest with wild red hair that circled his head like a crown of thorns silently thanked the almighty Lord above when his elbow connected with Franz's ribs.

Franz turned away and slipped the mouth of a flask between his lips.

Over Franz's objections, Doctor Hermann Artz had scampered away claiming he had other patients to tend. There was nothing more he could do to aid the Countess and feared that upon her passing the Count would order his head on the block. A nurse dressed in white fidgeted and wrung her hands at the foot of Anna's bed. She stared at the patient and prayed inaudibly that the Count might not order her jailed for failing to reverse the pre-ordained. Manfred, the Count's manservant, waited stiff-backed by the bedroom door, willing his tears not to flow. Oh, how he loved the Countess, an Aphrodite in a castle of Titans. The servant boys Raimund and Simon huddled to the side of the bedroom suite, primed to spring forth at another snarl from their Count. Fetch a pillow. Get water. Find another doctor. More blood. Throughout Stuppach Castle, members of the Freemasons and contemporaries of the Von Walsegg family sipped clove tea, spoke in hushed tones, and awaited the news of the inevitable. Servants of the castle, doorkeepers, gardeners, cooks, valets, ushers, the hunt master, and the castle dwarf worked glumly as they awaited news of their mistress's demise. Outside, it seemed, all the citizens of Gloggnitz, Austria huddled in sub-freezing temperature and prayed for a miracle.

In Anna's bedroom, Franz sobbed. "Don't let her die, Father."

Franz didn't want to lose his young wife, especially on this day as her death would interfere with his attendance at the public flogging to be held tomorrow. The thrashing was sure to be entertaining. Men caught in flagrante delicto were made to do the most embarrassing and hilarious things. How would it look if twenty-four hours after Anna's death he was whooping and hollering like a drunken bachelor? He could mandate the date of the flogging be changed, but then he'd have to delay his pleasure. If only he had the power to alter the date of his wife's expiry. Another project he'd have to work on in his secret lab.

At her bedside, Mattheus wrestled with his own tears. "Take me." The words barely floated from his lips. He wished he and Anna were alone. "Take one thousand men instead, Lord." He eyed the wedding ring on Anna's left hand and grimaced. The large diamond was flamboyant and unsuited for the understated Anna. Certainly not what the priest would have chosen to adorn her long, delicate finger if Anna had been his bride.

The von Flammbergins, Anna's family, had been active members in the Schottwien Parish Church since Mattheus was a priestling over thirty years ago. He had been present at Anna's birth, watched her grow from infant to curious child to sweet teen to stunning adult. When the marriage of Anna von Flammbergin to Count Franz von Walsegg was negotiated, Mattheus ached to tell her parents what a mistake they had made. Anna deserved a man who was honorable in more than name alone. Not Franz, whose ego was as large as the many estates he owned; not Franz, who claimed to love his young wife while he visited the brothel on the other side of the Danube weekly; not Franz, who cautioned Anna not to speak with another man unless related by blood. Fortunately, Mattheus, as a servant of God, was an exception to the Count's rule.

Shortly after she and Franz married, Mattheus noticed bruises in the crux of Anna's arms. He asked her about them one morning as they prepared for the Feast of Our Lady the Martyr. She blushed with embarrassment as if underplaying the beauty of a diamond bracelet.

"That's just Franz."

Mattheus pointed at her arms. His hand shook. "D-D-Did he do that?"

"He has quirks."

"Quirks?"

"Well, he, uh..." She lowered her voice even though they were alone. "He's obsessed with blood. It's part of his medical experiments."

He took her wrists in his chunky fingers and examined the underside of her forearms.

She pulled her arms from his grip and clasped her hands behind her back. "It's nothing that concerns you."

From then on, Anna wore long sleeves.

At her bedside, with minutes, perhaps seconds remaining in the life of Countess Anna, Mattheus viewed her arms. The marks and bruises from where Franz had drawn blood were mostly healed.

"Do something, Father," Franz ordered.

The priest viewed the wedding band again, symbolic of all he could never be, could never have. He longed to be a loving and trusted husband who earned an honest wage with his hands, a real man who after a hard day's work drank lager with the boys at the local pub and then went home to a hot meal and a willing wife. But that had never been his path, not when fifty years ago, only hours after his birth on Christmas Eve, he was abandoned in a manger, taken to a convent, and raised by nuns who disciplined him for the smallest infractions with slashes from a studded, leather strap.

"Open your eyes, Sweet Anna, so we can see each other one last time." Mattheus urged.

Her breath slowed.

"Nurse! Do something." Franz yelled.

The nurse ran to her side but Mattheus pushed her away. He bent and put his lips on Anna's mouth. Not to resuscitate her—he knew that was not possible—but to steal her final breath.

"Get off." Franz grabbed his shoulder.

Mattheus used his corpulence to maintain his position. It would take more than Franz to get him off her. Twenty Lipizzaners wouldn't be sufficient.

His lips on Anna's, he inhaled the remaining warmth from her being. Her eyes opened. Mattheus pulled back. In a flash of clarity and forgiveness, she looked to her priest and toward her husband. She breathed in the lavender incenses, allowed the candle flames to dance across her pupils, and soaked in her final visions of the Persian tapestries and handcrafted Turkish furniture that decorated her room.

Franz pulled at Mattheus. The vicar was not to be moved.

Anna's eyes wandered in nystagmus. Her lips moved.

The priest shifted his ear to her lips. "What, my love?"

"Oskar," she said.

"Raimund. Simon." Franz yelled. "Remove him."

Hands grabbed at his back, clutched the rolls of his stomach, and pulled at his side meat. A forearm clasped around his neck. They beat their fists on the priest's back and shoulders, pulled his hair, and bit the fleshy skin on his arms. The skinny Raimund and the feminine Simon added little leverage to Franz's cause. What he felt, gave him pleasure.

"Who is Oskar?" he whispered to Anna.

Her eyes blanked. Her final breath gusted. The stale smell from her tongue turned floral. As a priest who witnessed hundreds, perhaps thousands, pass into the loving arms of God, he was familiar with Anna's transition and her rebirth into eternal life. Breath turns fresh, skin vibrates with the pink tingle of a newborn's flesh, muscles release. Death, a loving parent who vows to shelter forever.

Franz punched Mattheus in the kidney. Weakened by Anna's death, the blow cut though the priest's core. He fell back to the floor. Franz collapsed on to Anna.

On all fours, Mattheus prayed. "Please, Lord, bring forth my rebirth and unite me with my sweet Anna. But first reveal, who is Oskar?"

Chapter Two

In the studio behind the home Oskar Glasman shared with his wife Hedy, sand, lime and plant ash cooked inside a steel and brick oven. Alone, Oskar recited his father's lessons. "An oak wood fire burns at 900 degrees. Lava liquefies at 1,300 degrees. Flesh melts at 1,400 degrees."

He waited for the furnace to exceed 2000 degrees Fahrenheit, the minimum temperature when glass melts and cullet—flecks of raw, clear glass—formed. Like glassblowers since the First Century B.C., Oskar stared into the flames and anticipated the precise moment to attach the melted glass to a pipe.

He tucked his long, curly hair, so blond it was almost white, behind his ears. He stepped toward the furnace and checked the temperature. With the pads of his fingers thickly covered with callouses, and nerves deadened from burns, he barely felt the heat. He read the temperature by the feel of the warmth that caressed his cheeks, by the sight of the hue of the red and orange flames, and by the sounds of the hisses and snaps.

He placed his hands on his lower back and stretched. The pain in his back worsened. *Damn these breasts.* He thought of the public flogging set for the following afternoon. Sadness overcame him. All citizens of Gloggnitz were required to attend per edict of Count Franz von Walsegg.

Hinges to the door of the studio creaked.

"Your assistant is here," Hedy announced.

He turned and smiled, a wide grin that spread across his face only upon the sight of two women: Hedy, his stunning wife, and Countess Anna von Walsegg, his closest friend.

Oskar and Anna were an unlikely duo, the Countess and the glassblower, the luminary and the sideshow. It was a display of Hedy's character that she never felt threatened by Oskar's relationship with the Countess. Now, Anna was gravely ill. He could not be by her side as their friendship had been secret. If the Count learned of their bond, gruesome consequences were certain.

"Perfect timing." He bent and kissed his wife, so exquisite and petite. "Ready?"

"At your service, Sire." She curtsied and smiled slyly.

Oskar ignored the binding around his chest that pinched his skin and pulled her into him. Warmth surged between his legs. The flush of his cheeks no longer from the heat of the oven.

"Is the furnace too hot?" Hedy teased.

How she flirted and still wanted him with as much vigor as if it were their wedding day three years prior. Oskar forced himself to separate from the small curves of her hips, from her tight stomach, and from her breasts that perfectly fit in his hands. Like a volcano about to erupt, the furnace bellowed.

Inside the oven, molten glass bubbled and flowed. He placed one end of a hollow metal pipe into the kiln, and twirled the blowpipe to gather glass. He loved this part, gathering the gather, the glass that stuck to the end of the pipe. It all began with the gather. Every fine glass sculpture depended upon the success of the gather like a fine morning suit began with the right cloth.

Heat from the metal rod singed his fingertips as he twirled the pipe. When he determined to have the right amount of molten glass snaked around the end of the blowpipe, he removed the rod from the furnace and rested it on a stand where he could stretch and manipulate the orange glowing glass. Using jacks that resembled large metal tweezers, he pulled on the heated glass, made an indent a few inches from the top, and formed distinction between haunches and back legs. He twirled the rod continuously, gyrating the blowpipe so the glass didn't settle. He rested the rod on a yoke to be able to slide the glass back into the furnace through the glory hole to reheat when the glass became less malleable.

He picked up a metal paddle to smooth and shape the hot figurine and angled the jacks to pull on it. Using industrial metal scissors, he pulled on the opposite end of the figure and formed a neck.

"Now," he said.

Hedy placed another blowpipe into the furnace, gathered glass and then gingerly attached the orange glowing blob to the neck of the figure on the end of Oskar's rod. Using the scissors, Oskar cut Hedy's pipe free from the glass and, utilizing the jacks again, formed the head of the horse, followed by its nose, eyes and ears.

"Again," Oskar instructed.

Hedy dipped the blowpipe back in the furnace and emerged with another hot gather, which she placed delicately along the neck of the horse. Oskar again cut the molten glass from Hedy's pipe, leaving behind the initial form of the horse's mane. Using the scissors, Oskar cut flowing lines into the mane. He put the horse back in the furnace and twirled the rod. The ache in his back heightened.

He removed the horse from the oven. "Let's go again."

Hedy heated more glass on her pipe, which Oskar then attached to the front of the horse. He cut its rear from his rod and attached its tail. Finished, he cut the horse loose from the blowpipe and, with gloved hands, placed it in the annealer, a separate oven used to gradually cool and harden the glass so it didn't crack or break as it solidified.

He took off the gloves, wiped sweat from his forehead and wrapped his hands around Hedy's waist. He kissed the tip of her nose and wiped perspiration from her cheeks.

"Anna is going to love it. It's a beautiful gift from you."

"From us," he corrected.

"I am only your assistant."

"You have helped me enough times you can create amazing sculptures on your own." He looked longingly at the annealer, as if he could see behind its iron door to the horse that glowed within. He sat on a stool, and relieved some of the pressure in his back. "I'm afraid Anna will never see the horse."

"Maybe she'll recover like she did last time."

The creak of the rusty hinges to the studio turned their sights to the door. Oskar's heart dipped at the vision of the slumping shoulders of the tall and muscular boy. At fifteen years old, Raimund was six years younger than Oskar. Pointed cheekbones carved his boyish face. Thick blond hair bopped over his eyes.

Oskar never cared which boy-servant the Count sent to deliver a message. Whether it was girl-obsessed Raimund who stared too long at Hedy, or sixteen-year-old Simon who was not as handsome as Raimund but better groomed, politer, and effeminate. Intrigued by both boys, Oskar learned something from each. From Raimund, he studied what it meant to be sexy, cavalier, whimsical, and how to strut without fear. From Simon, he took note of chivalry, vulnerability, grace, and feminine masculinity.

Raimund stepped into the studio. A grim expression burdened his face.

"Is she...?" Hedy grabbed Oskar's arm for support.

Oskar looked to his hands, imagined he held the Countess' face in them, saw the way her lips moved, heard her kind words. His throat tightened and his eyes stung. *Be a man. Don't cry.* He looked to the annealer where Anna's horse cooled, saddened he would not get to present it to her. *Don't show emotion. Don't let on to Raimund the devastation I feel.*

"Does the Count wish me to make something for her memorial service?" Oskar managed.

"Not that I am aware. She will be buried in the morning."

Oskar lowered his head. Hedy slipped her fingers into the crux of her husband's arm. Raimund scanned Hedy's body. He did not look away when Oskar's eyes met his.

Raimund bowed. "I must return to the castle before the Count notices I'm missing."

"Wait," Oskar said. "The flogging tomorrow, will the date be changed out of respect for the Countess?" *Please let it be cancelled.*

"The Count said it must go on in honor of the Countess."

"In honor?" Oskar said. "She never sanctioned these horrible events. She abhorred them." Oskar stopped when he realized Raimund stared at him. Hedy's grip tightened on Oskar's arm. "I mean," Oskar retreated, "I believe Countess Anna disapproved. I have no way of really knowing."

"Yes, right. Well, it's a sad time in Gloggnitz."

"That it is," Hedy said.

Raimund backed out of the studio. His eyes traveled along the curve of Hedy's hips before he turned and trotted back to Stuppach Castle.

Chapter Three
February 15, 1791

On 14 February 1791 died at Schloss Stuppach and was interred here in the family crypt on the 15th the high and nobly born Countess Anna von Walsegg, nee von Flammbergin, her 20th year, celebrated by me, Mattheus Richter, deacon and priest.

Father Mattheus put the quill down, waited for the ink to dry, and closed the large record book. The red vellum cover clamped on the lined pages. A cloud of dust curled into the frigid air. He refused to allow the nuns to clean the Book of the Departed, preferring instead to watch the powdery dirt rise and disappear as if transporting the soul of the latest scribed name to heaven.

Mattheus pulled his brown thick woolen frock around his shoulders. It was colder inside the medieval stone walls of the Schottwien Parish Church than outside.

What else should I write about Anna?

He picked up the quill and dipped it into an ink jar he had placed on the pew next to him and mused, "Who was Countess Anna?"

Images cascaded around his brain. The genuine memories filled him with tedium. The fantasies stirred his longing.

"Best to keep those to myself."

He bent over the Book of the Departed and wrote. *A noble creature buried this morning in a most beautiful ceremony.*

She excelled at knitting and archery. Loved horses, especially the Lipizzaners. Charitable. My beautiful love.

He dipped the quill in ink again and, with a heavy hand, blotted out the last three words.

He added, *Cause of death: Acute Putrid Fever.* He placed the quill down, fanned the page so the ink would dry, closed the book again and positioned it on the pew next to him.

He leaned back and clasped his hands on his belly. Anna's last breath, the one he had ingested, swirled within him. She ran through his blood and settled in his groin. His breathing quickened. *Anna. My dear lovely beautiful Anna.* He put the Book on his lap, to cover his sin.

Her final word crept into his solace and his eyes shot open. *Oskar.* Who was Oskar?

He knew everyone in the small mountain region of Gloggnitz, a village surrounded by Mount Rax and Mount Schneeberg, two able sentries. There was only one Oskar, yet it couldn't be *that* Oskar who had consumed her ultimate thought.

Mattheus had searched for another Oskar and had inquired of the mourners who waited inside Stuppach Castle and those who camped outside. He tried to be casual when he asked the male servants if they knew an Oskar other than the glassblower. Anna had no relatives baptized Oskar that he knew of and he believed he knew everything about her. He inquired with stealth, asked everyone but Franz who was so distraught the only thing he heeded was that devil alcohol. Mattheus was certain Franz had not heard Anna's ultimate syllables. He was fraught with fear to share the name with him, confident every Oskar from Gloggnitz to Vienna would be tortured.

Had Oskar been Anna's secret lover? Mattheus laughed at the thought of Anna and Oskar's naked bodies intertwined.

Never would Anna have allowed that union to occur, and if Franz learned about it he surely would have put Oskar to death and Anna in seclusion.

"Father."

Mattheus kept his eyes focused on the Book, the tome heavy in his frocked and wide lap. He wanted to delay the sight and smell that would soon come upon him. The priest knew, even before he looked up, even before he got close to Franz, that the widower of Countess Anna reeked of liquor, grime and halitosis. Franz had been drunk ever since Doctor Artz announced there was no more he could do to aid the Countess.

Mattheus placed the book on the bench and stood. The Count teetered in the church's center aisle. Wooden pews on either side were ready to catch Franz should he fall.

"Why don't you sit?"

Blood vessels on Franz's cheeks blemished his aristocratic pale skin. Tiny veins spread like webs. Thick dark hair grew to his broad shoulders. His chin was square and strong, his eyes piercing and light blue as if etched from stained glass. A black cloak hung loosely off one shoulder. Despite the chill, alcohol steamed from Franz's body.

Knowing feelings of envy and jealousy were sins, Mattheus tried not to compare his own barrel-shaped stomach, short stature and red frizzed hair to that of the lean, tall and usually well-appointed Count.

"How can I help you?" Mattheus inquired.

"I've come to take Anna home."

"She is home. She is with God."

"I know the truth about you and your God," Franz slurred. "He doesn't exist, and you, Father, are a fraud. If He was real, He would not have taken my wife."

"She's at peace now." Mattheus tried to speak gently, paternally.

"At peace in that crypt?" He spit the word crypt like a tumor launched from his tongue. "That is not where she belongs. Her home is with me." Franz lurched forward and dropped to his knees. He grabbed at the priest's frock, looked up at him, and cried. "Why, Father? Why was she taken? We'd been married not even four years."

"Come, my son, pray with me." Mattheus sat in a pew and reached for the Count's arm.

Franz recoiled. "If I cannot touch my Anna, I will not touch or be touched by another."

"You are a young man. You will love again."

"I am twenty-eight years old and I will never be with another woman. I demand you release her to me."

"Her journey is inscribed in the Book of Life. You cannot change it."

Mattheus tried not to holler at the pathetic, inebriated lump at his feet. He wanted to order him to stand like a man and stop acting like he had ever treated Anna as more than a showpiece. Franz had possessed Anna in the same way he had idolized the expensive and rare art he collected and the musical compositions he pretended to arrange.

Franz stood, wobbled, wiped his eyes and straightened his cloak. He staggered and sat with a thud next to the priest.

"I need to take her home."

Mattheus tried not to wretch from the assault of alcohol fumes. "I know, my son, but she's already interred. You agreed she should be laid to rest in the family crypt and that it be done immediately. "

"I was drunk with grief."

"You will be with her again one day. We all will."

"I need her now."

Despite his deep dislike for the Count, pity overcame the priest. Franz was powerful on the outside, adrift on the inside.

Franz withdrew a flask from under his cloak and flung the liquid down his throat.

He threw the silver canteen onto a pew, stumbled along the church aisle and toward the front wood door. Stuppach Castle wasn't far, maybe two kilometers away. It was late afternoon, the hour before the horizon dimmed. Mattheus considered telling James, the church groundskeeper, to escort the Count home, but decided against it. If along the way to the castle the Count fell into the Danube, or met with bandits who became too free with a blade, the priest would shed nary a tear. Not real ones, at least.

Franz exited the church and the priest looked to the rafters. "Shame on me for having thoughts of a man being harmed, even a man like that." Mattheus threw himself to his knees and looked up at statues of Jesus and his four disciples. "Please forgive me, Holy Father, for my wicked, wicked thoughts. I must be punished." He reached for a thick rawhide belt tucked under a front pew, and pushed his frock off. Bare chested and bare backed, he was protected only by the curly red hair that carpeted him. Each blow from the leather cinch on his back, his chest, his arms and legs, felt to be a feverish thunderbolt. Patches of skin bloodied and bubbled and floated to the ground like swatches of cloth.

He counted fifteen whacks. The pain worsened with each. Weeping and weakened, he laid the whip on the ground, rose into a pew, and clasped his hands in front of him.

Breathless, he managed, "Thank you, Lord, for the pleasure of this pain. Thank you, Lord, for punishing my evil thoughts."

He hid the belt under the bench, a sleeping snake until the next time when his thoughts proved him to be more a disciple of Satan than a servant of God. He thought of the rose-colored small silk satchel he kept in his room in the back of the church. Yes, there would be a next time.

He rested his face in his hands and savored the ache of the deep, throbbing wounds. A different thunderbolt jolted him and his rotted soul felt suddenly renewed. He was energized and holy and imagined his blood that dripped onto the wood bench to be the blood of Christ.

"Hey, get away from there." James yelled from outside the church walls.

The priest raised his head and heard sounds of scuffling, men arguing, wood breaking, the clank of metal on stone. Knowing he ought to mediate the dispute, he pulled his frock around him, glad it was sewn from dark brown wool as his blood blended well into the fabric. He wore dark clothes and never allowed the damaged and scarred parts of his body to be exposed for public view. He refused to permit the nuns to wash his cloaks in the Danube, claiming it was a ritual he must perform personally.

With much effort, as every muscle ached and groaned, he plodded toward the front door of the church. He stepped into the frosty air and into the shadow of the church bell tower. Cold slapped at his wounds.

"What is going on?" Mattheus demanded.

There was no need for an answer since the story unfolded in front of him. The beginning, the middle, and how this would end. Chips of white stone covered Franz's face, his cape, and his black pants. Behind Franz, the low, wood fence around the von Walsegg family crypt was toppled. Much of the stone front of the crypt had been smashed.

James panted. "I tried to stop him."

Franz raised a sledgehammer over his head.

"Put that down," Mattheus yelled.

"Stay away, Father." He swung the mallet through the air.

The weight of the tool knocked the Count off balance. He fell and awkwardly got to his feet. He banged the hammer against the crypt. Chips of stone flew.

James moved to stop him.

Mattheus grabbed the groundskeeper and pulled him away.

Franz dug at the dirt with his hands and whacked at the stone. Dirt and rock ricocheted around him.

The smell of the earth and the tang of the underworld hung in the chill.

"What will happen with Anna once you get her home?" Mattheus called.

The Count paused and looked to the priest. "She will live forever."

Chapter Four

Early evening, Oskar and Hedy stood at the back of the crowd. Snow fell. Despite the hundreds of people between them and the stage, the high platform was fully visible. All the townspeople were required to attend unless too old or feeble. Failure to appear was punished by twenty-seven whacks with a leather strap, more for repeat offenders. General Inspector Adalwolf Recht administered the punishment at the orders of the Count.

Oskar recognized most in the crowd. Heinrich Müller, the miller, stood near Abraham Schneider, the tailor, who idle talked with Edgar Fischer, the fisherman, and Gaston Weber, the weaver. Teachers and children were there. Schools were closed and would be the following day too since this was sure to be a late night of celebration. Shop owners were present. Businesses were dark. Whores fidgeted to the side and waved to customers. Husbands hoped wives didn't notice. A few wives hoped their husbands didn't notice too.

Father Mattheus climbed a wooden staircase to the stage. He held a large red book with the word Bible stamped on its cover. Anna's funeral had been that morning and had been for family members only, and so this moment was for the town to mourn the loss of their Countess together. The pastor spoke and fingered the book but never opened it. Oskar listened half-heartedly. No one knew Anna as he had and so the priest's words meant little to him. Oskar would find a way to honor his Anna. At least, he thought as he scanned the crowd, Franz had the decency to not attend this horrid event. Maybe he truly was mourning their loss. Had Oskar misjudged the man?

Hedy shivered and snuggled close to him. He put his arm around her and drew her into his side. It was ridiculous to have this public event at all, but to hold it in the middle of February was absurd. To not cancel it in honor of Anna's passing was insulting. With the Count's blessing, Recht probably salivated at having caught the homosexuals in the act and couldn't wait to show off his find like a fisherman who displayed a bloody catch.

Oskar knew the men but had never spoken with them beyond a friendly greeting. They were about his age, churchgoers, from good families, and dedicated to their studies. They had been caught in a supply closet in Gaston Weber's store. One of the men was the weaver's nephew and believed they had found a safe place for their tryst. Sadly, they were mistaken.

The General Inspector caught them himself. A big prize for Recht who, it was believed, was tipped off by Gaston Weber himself. Seems the boys had been sneaking into the weaver's shop since they were teenagers and Gaston had asked them to stop. Getting in the good graces of the General Inspector might mean Weber would not have to pay such high taxes.

Father Mattheus said a final prayer for Anna and descended the steps off the stage. His heavy feet took him toward the church. The pastor was not required to attend these occasions, other than to say the opening prayer.

Recht snapped a whip. The crowd cheered. He climbed the stairs and silenced them with waves of his hands.

"Bring the prisoners forth." He barked.

Naked and shackled around their ankles, waists and wrists, Ernst Weber and Hulbert Lang stumbled up the staircase to center stage. They shook from fear and cold. They pleaded for their lives.

"Don't watch," Hedy whispered.

The Glasmans had perfected this maneuver. Their heads raised as if attentive, their eyes downcast or looking to the sides so they didn't have to see the humility and torture Ernst and Hulbert were to undergo. Neither Oskar nor Hedy had figured out how not to hear the screams.

Dr. Artz stood near the stage and clutched a medical bag. He wouldn't need any of its contents, only the tips of his fingers to determine when the boys no longer had pulses. The undertaker waited nearby with two newly made wood caskets stacked on a horse driven carriage.

In the distance, a hunched back figure, cloaked in black, carried a heavy load through the driving snow. Stuppach Castle rose in the distance like a newly forming shadow.

Chapter Five

Franz cradled Anna's decomposing body and hurried uphill toward Stuppach Castle. His knee-high leather boots padded along the dirt road that was covered with snow. Anna's fine skin shaded green on her face and purple-gray on her arms. Having been buried in her wedding dress, the white silk and lace were singed grayish brown and caked with mud. The back of her dress was soiled with dried feces. Bacteria overtook her organs, and emitted a foul gas. Her usual lavender scent absent among the stench of rot. Her eyes protruded.

From atop the hill, Mattheus saw the mass gathered in the public square not too far from the church. Franz no longer felt regret for missing the flogging and the other fun Recht had in store for those fairy boys, not when he cradled Anna. The Count had only one chance to be with Anna again. There would be other opportunities to witness floggings, especially like the one happening now. Men have been lying with men since the beginning of time. Public embarrassment, whippings, even death have never been deterrents. Later, he would get a play-by-play of the goings-on from his favorite whore.

He looked over his shoulder and back toward Schottwien Parish Church to make sure Father Mattheus did not follow. He slowed as he realized the priest probably tended to James and the wounds Franz had inflicted upon him, and then had to rush to say the benediction for the flogging. He had been so desperate to remove Anna from the crypt he had swung the hammer with passion. The opening chorus of Bach's *Mass in B*

Minor played in the background of his mind as the mallet connected with James's back, arms and legs. He might have done real harm to the old man. Still, he didn't have time to care about a lowly church worker. He was bringing Anna home.

He rushed down the street; the church several blocks in his past, bringing Anna back to life and still in his future. Thatched roofs and wood doors of one-story homes greeted him on either side like a saluting army. The upper levels of Stuppach Castle, four-storeys in all, rose in the distance. Its fine red roof reigned over Gloggnitz, and its many windows shone in the setting sun. On a clear day, the castle could be seen from Vienna and the lower rising servants' quarters, barn and silo could be viewed from ten kilometers away.

He managed to pull his cloak closer to ward off the winter's wind. The small flakes of snow moved with more ferocity and grew, suggesting the accumulation would be large. What a perfect time to be snowed in as he had much work to do. He tucked his chin into his chest and barreled on, a black hunched figure plowing through a white blaze with a lifeless form in his arms.

He never should have given consent for Anna to be buried in the Walsegg family crypt. When she had first been diagnosed by Dr. Artz, Franz's indifference swirled. Wealthy and handsome, he would find a woman younger and prettier than Anna to be his next wife. Besides, Anna had been baulking at being the object of his experiments. She forbade him from drawing her blood and refused his requests to collect her urine, feces and skin samples. He thought to punish her, but the obedient sixteen-year-old he had married had grown into an obstinate adult. While he was enraged at her inappropriate behavior, he was also awed. As her illness grew grave and he realized he would lose her, he was surprised by the sadness that overcame him and sought solace from drink. In his entire life, nothing had ever been taken from him. No fight lost, no object of desire withheld, no lust unrequited. As she grew sicker, so did his petulance. Now that she was gone, he was outraged.

How dare she be taken from me!

His pace slowed. He breathed through his mouth to avoid the stench. The ground grew slick and he recalled carrying her over the threshold to their bedroom on their wedding night. He had lifted her other times too. Into the bedroom for romantic encounters, over puddles of water and mud so as not to ruin her shoes or dress, onto riding horses, and into carriages. But now, she seemed heavier. No, he rationalized, that wasn't possible. How could she weigh more when the mass of life had been stolen from her body? Didn't life weigh more than death? In death her arms did not warmly cradle his neck, her legs did not scissor-kick flirtatiously, and her head did not tilt back in laughter. Instead, her arms drooped by her sides, her legs hung over his forearm with the heaviness of tree limbs, and her head flopped with each step he took. Not only that, but her eyes were open and vacant, her mouth agape, her tongue swollen and black. Maggots festered in her mouth, ears, and nostrils.

He looked to the castle in the near-distance. Stuppach Castle belonged to his family since 1659, purchased with riches garnered over one hundred and thirty years ago. Since the Walsegg family moved into *Schloss Stuppach* many changes had been made. An indoor chapel was added by Franz's great-grandfather. His grandfather updated the thirty guestrooms and forty-two bathrooms with the finest silk and gold. The estate gardens had been redesigned by his Father. Franz's mother had overseen renovations of the main kitchen, the three smaller kitchens and the six dining rooms in preparation for Pope Pius VI's visit in March 1782 on his way to Vienna. When Franz became lord of the castle shortly after the

Pope's visit, he made two changes. He built a chamber where he and his friends played and enjoyed classical music and he added a secret underground laboratory.

The fast falling snow covered the walkways when Franz reached the front gardens of Stuppach. The wind and the driving snow fell sideways into his eyes and pelted Anna. His intestines cramped from the cold. He stepped onto the long path leading to the front door and slipped. He clutched Anna to his chest, unable to break his fall with his hands lest he drop her.

He landed with a thud on his right hip. "*Gottverdammt.*"

Franz lay on the ground, Anna on top of him, his hip on fire. He slid from under her, crouched, placed one arm under her shoulders and another under her knees, and prepared to hoist her to finish their journey. Her left hand fell onto his leg.

"*Was ist das?*" He brought her hand closer to his face and blinked away cascading snow.

He looked at her hand from different angles. No matter how he viewed his dead wife's hand, it looked the same. The fourth finger on her left hand had been removed.

"She died with ten fingers," Franz said.

Despite the cold and the snow, his face turned red as if afire. Missing along with her ring finger was her wedding band.

Chapter Six

Franz made no eye contact when he entered the castle, not with the butlers nor with the maids. He hastily carried Anna through the maze of hallways and rooms. Near the library, he stopped in front of a closed door. Manfred stood straight-backed to the side of the door. A padlock barred entry.

Franz balanced Anna on his knees. He withheld curses as his hip seared with pain. "Is there ice in the box?"

"Yes, as you requested." He bowed.

Fifty-two years as a valet showed in Manfred's rounded shoulders and downcast eyes. He would turn seventy in a few days. Perhaps if he had been the domestic of a different member of the Von Walsegg family—anyone other than Franz whom he had served for the last nine years—he would feel sprier and would not pray daily for his master's demise.

He looked at Anna, slumped in Franz's arms. "She is starting to smell a little rancid, wouldn't you say?"

"Open it," the Count ordered.

Manfred withdrew a long thin gold key from the breast pocket of his tailored suit and unlocked the bolt. He opened the door and stepped out of the way.

With a grunt, Franz lifted her and stepped inside the short landing. "Don't let anybody in. Do not leave lest I require your service."

"*Ja, mein Herr*." Manfred closed the door.

Swathed in darkness, Franz stepped forward and counted as he descended the stairs. Forty-one until he and Anna reached the bottom. He did not notice the temperature dipped. He was too hot and too excited to feel the cold. Even the pain in his hip dissipated.

He arranged Anna on a raised metal gurney and lit a taper candle. He went around the room that was the size of a study and added fire to tapers, pillars and votives. The rest of the castle had electricity but not here. His laboratory was to be lit only by flames.

Franz circled Anna. Her eyes followed him, he was sure of it. Was that a seductive smile on her lips? Was she flirting with him?

He ran a finger along her jaw and over her lips. "Always playing the coy one, my dear. It is clear a fire for your husband still burns."

He threw off his cloak and mounted her. Her body bucked underneath his as he pushed his trousers down. He was already hard, had been the whole walk home. This would be their last time together as husband and wife. The last time she would fulfill her duty. He spread her legs and entered her. Her body moved rhythmically with his. He came quickly, perhaps the fastest ever with Anna beneath him or any whore for that matter.

Spent, he collapsed on top of her. "Am I too heavy?"

He climbed off the gurney and pulled on a white lab coat. He tugged black rubber gloves over his hands and wheeled a wood cart to where Anna waited.

On the cart was a wood box finely constructed from Austrian Pine. He opened the lid and his gloved hand hovered above three knives of varying blade lengths—five, seven and nine inches—and over scalpels suitable for amputation of fingers, hands or feet. A capital saw lined up next, proper for amputation of larger limbs such as the leg above the knee. On the sides of the red velvet lined case were forceps, needles and surgical thread made from catgut. A tourniquet and two hand trephines completed the contents of the kit.

Bottles of Nitrous Oxide and Ether were stacked on shelves near the freezer compartment Manfred had packed with ice.

Franz studied Anna's motionless face, disappointed she offered no expression of gratitude. Didn't he deserve better than that from his wife? Hadn't he just provided her pleasure? Wasn't he about to give her the ultimate gift of immortality?

"Well," he reasoned, "at least you won't need anesthetics."

He despised screams of agony and feared others might hear even though the walls of the lab were soundproof. It was difficult to find sedatives that lasted long enough for him to complete some of his tasks. Many of his subjects had awakened during procedures, only to have the Count employ drastic measures, sometimes deadly measures, to quiet them.

He lifted one of the trephines from the surgical box. Used for trepanning, a procedure to drill a hole in the skull to extract blood, the tool had been forged from metal and had a pin in the center of a cylindrical blade. His heart pounded with excitement as if he listened to Mozart's *The Magic Flute*. Wolfgang was still composing the two-act opera but he had played a piece of it for Franz. It was set to premiere at the *Wiednertheater* in Vienna at the end of the year.

"Too bad you will miss it, my love." Franz kissed her forehead and ignored the maggots that wiggled in the crevices of her once beautiful face. "Wolfgang will surely outdo himself."

Trepanning relieved pressure and drained blood from the brain on the living. But in Franz's operating room, trepanning served a different function. He tilted the gurney down so Anna's head was lower than the rest of her body. He waited several moments. His exhilaration built. It was hard to be patient but he knew he had to do this right. Perhaps they would write about him in medical journals. His accomplishments preserved for centuries.

He snapped on a surgical mask and hat and pulled out a wood bucket from a bottom shelf. He placed the bucket under Anna's head and began to drill behind her left ear. Blood drained from the hole and into the bucket. When there was no more blood to be removed, he poured the thick red fluid into several glass jars and stacked them in the freezer. Blood froze below twenty-eight degrees Fahrenheit.

He shifted the table so her feet were the lowest point and, using the smallest knife, cut holes in her feet. Blood drained into the bucket. He repeated this procedure by tilting her in other directions and cutting holes in her body. Methodically, he transferred the blood to glass jars, which he then piled in the freezer.

When there was no more blood to be drained, he took out the saw. It wasn't easy cutting through bone, especially large bones like the femur, but he was strong and relished the opportunity to feel close to his Anna one last time. This was, he knew, his last chance to make love to her in the most intimate way, by dismantling her, by loving every part of her, her blood, her bones, each organ, every vein and artery.

He threw out her fat—there hadn't been much anyway—and ground her organs and muscles as small as seasoning. He cleaned the bones in a deep sink and stored them in the freezer, along with her hair, the tendons of her jaw, and the anvil and stirrup bones of her middle ear. He held her teeth in the palm of his hand and jiggled them like pebbles to be tossed into a stream. Euphoria entombed him. A freedom never experienced, as if he could take flight into a moonlit sky and soar above the Danube, over Austria, over the world.

He put her teeth in the pocket of his pants, threw off the bloodied and soiled surgical hat, mask and lab coat, and dropped them to the floor. His boots were filthy too, as were the bottoms of his pants that had not been covered by the lab coat. He didn't care. He ran up the forty-one steps and opened the door. Manfred leaned against the wall. His eyes closed and his shoulders slumped with fatigue.

Franz had been in the lab for ten hours. The sun had risen.

Manfred straightened. "*Ja, mein Herr.*"

"Send Raimund to summon Oskar," the Count said.

Chapter Seven

February 16, 1791

A heavy snowfall blanketed Gloggnitz. Oskar and Hedy spooned. The first rays of the morning sun streamed through a crack in a curtain and cast a rainbow on their bedspread. Oskar fought to keep the sounds of Ernst and Hulbert's torture out of his head.

Strong raps on the heavy wood front door startled them. Oskar sat up.

"Who…?" Hedy asked.

"I'll find out."

He swung his feet off the bed. A whip of cold slapped at him. His bare feet struck the chilled ground. His lower back ached.

The knocking resumed.

"Oskar," Raimund called, "the Count needs you."

The glassblower wrapped his nightdress closer around him and shuffled toward the front door. He leaned his cheek against the door. "I will be to Stuppach Castle soon, Raimund."

"Count von Walsegg demanded I escort you personally."

"I must get dressed. I will be a few minutes behind you." Oskar knew that was a lie as it would take more than a few minutes for him to dress. He would deal with the consequences of being tardy later.

"He said he would chop off all my toes if I do not bring you back swiftly."

Oskar sighed. The Count might do that to poor Raimund.

"Very well. I will be ready soon." He walked toward his dressing room.

"Oskar," Raimund called, "it's freezing out here."

Oskar hesitated. How would he explain to the Count that Raimund obtained frostbite because he would not invite him into his home? He opened the door and folded his arms tightly across his chest.

Raimund stepped in and extended his right hand.

Oskar kept his arms tightly clamped. "I'm too cold."

Raimund dropped his hand to his side and stomped the snow from his boots onto a thick blue and gold braided rug.

Oskar pointed his chin toward the sitting room. Next to a wood burning stove was a neatly arranged pile of wood cut several months ago in preparation for the long winter.

"Put those logs in the stove to warm up. The matches are over there." Oskar used his elbow as a pointer.

"*Vielen Dank, Mein Herr*." Thank you. "Is *Frau* Hedwig here?"

"She is sleeping. You will have to leer at my wife another time." He tried to sound good-natured.

Raimund smiled, a wide, boyish grin. "I hope to meet a woman as beautiful as Hedy one day."

"If you do, you will be the second luckiest man in the world. Go, start the fire, warm yourself."

Oskar left Raimund in the sitting room. His arms still folded against his chest, he walked toward the bedroom where Hedy snored softly, rhythmically.

Oskar tiptoed into the dressing room and stepped into the pan closet. He lifted the lid and stood over it, careful to pull his nightdress out of the way. He grabbed a glass funnel and positioned it between his legs. He peed into the chamber pot—which he had blown from glass—wiped himself with a rag, closed the lid and stepped out of the closet. Hedy would empty the pot later in the day.

In the dressing room, he stripped off his gown, let it fall to the floor, and tried to avert his eyes from the full-sized mirror Hedy insisted upon. He wished to never be witness to his reflection, not in a mirror, not in a pool of water, not in another person's eyes. But as much as he hoped to not see himself, he found it hard to look away.

In the mirror, his breasts were bulbous and hung to the bottom of his ribs. Dark blue veins crisscrossed his skin. His nipples were large and red and often erect, even without provocation. He wished he had been born with smaller breasts, or no breasts at all, and a boyish physique like Hedy's. Her breasts delicate and delightful. Her nipples tinted a lovely taupe and flat against her skin unless coaxed. The irony never left him. Delicate, feminine Hedy was more boyish in appearance than he.

He turned away, reached to a shelf and pulled out a bundle of thin, folded fabric, about three metres long. Without looking in the mirror, he put one end over his left breast, then his right, and around his back. He wrapped the fabric around and around and bound his breasts in an effort to make them disappear.

"Scheiß drauf!" Fuck.

It wasn't flat enough; the fabric was bulky. He unwound it, threw it off, and cursed his breasts. Tears formed in his eyes.

"Ein Mann." Oskar spoke to the strange body in the mirror. Be a man.

He inhaled deeply and placed the fabric around his chest again, watching this time in the mirror. He knew whatever he did was not going to be sufficient to hide his breasts under his clothes. It never was. It took a woman's touch to make him a man.

"Let me."

Hedy's sweet morning breath calmed him. He raised his arms over his head and closed his eyes. Her small adept hands unwrapped the fabric, and then fastened it again.

"There," Hedy said. "You can look now."

He opened his eyes. His were breasts perfectly bound with no bumps in the fabric. She pulled out a shirt and helped him into it.

"What did I do to deserve you?" He placed his hands on her waist. "What made you choose to live your life with a monster?"

"Don't talk like that Oskar Glasman. You know I don't like it. You are no monster."

"If others knew the truth, they would hunt me as if I were one."

She reached up and kissed the tip of his nose. "They will never find out. Now the vest." She steered his arms into it and slid the three buttons into their assigned slits.

"How do I look?" he asked, his back to the mirror.

She straightened his vest. "You look like the handsome man you are. Perhaps you would like to wear pants too?" She rose to her tippy toes again and their mouths met.

Chapter Eight

Twenty-two years ago in Vienna, Oskar was born a girl named Oskarina. He bawled when his parents, Alexander and Jana, dressed him in pink, and held his breath until he turned blue when they tried to coerce him to play with dolls. He was content to wear boys' clothes and to play with boys' toys. When he was called Oskarina and not Oskar, he threw himself to the floor and banged his forehead until he bled. A jagged scar on the side of his temple evidenced his childhood tantrums.

When he was nine years old, his parents decided it was too exhausting to make him be who he never would be. They moved ninety kilometers to Gloggnitz. They cut his hair short and tucked it behind his ears. He wore boys' jumpers and caps, was as good at sports as the other boys, and fancied girls. Introductions were made with Oskar as their son. They enrolled Oskar in school and joined Schottwien Parish Church. Only Father Mattheus knew the truth of the boy's identity. Alexander and Jana needed someone to confide in and who was safer than their pastor.

Further complications arose as Oskar reached puberty. Like his father he was tall. Like his mother he was curvaceous and well endowed. Schoolmates ridiculed him for being a boy with breasts and for having a round bottom. He refused to change for exercise class. Daily, his nose was bloodied, his ego was battered, and his tenacity was tested.

During his thirteenth year, he begged his parents to take him out of school. "I don't need to learn anything more about religion, math and music," he cried. "None of that is relevant to my life. I want to be like you, Papa, and like Opa too. Let me live up to our surname."

Alexander held out his hands, marred from decades of glassblowing. "We hoped you'd pursue philosophy so you don't end up like this. We hoped you'd be a man who earned a wage through his brain and not his hands."

"You want to lock me away at a university," Oskar argued. "You want me cloistered. If I were a girl, you'd commit me to an order to be a nun."

Their silence served as Oskar's confirmation.

"It will be a good life," his father finally spoke. His normally robust voice, soft and flat.

"It will be a safe life," his mother added.

"I don't want safe," Oskar said. "I want happy."

Two mornings later, he refused to leave his room. His classmates had locked him in a storage closet the previous day and the teacher didn't look for him until it was almost suppertime. He was not only teased and bullied by the other children, he was irrelevant to his teacher.

"Please don't make me go back," he cried.

Alexander and Jana badly wanted their only child to be fulfilled. They let him stay home from school and took him to a fair. Maybe a little fun would help them see things more clearly.

At the fair, with his parents on either side, Oskar stared at a carousel with wood-carved and jeweled horses, lions, zebras and giraffes. The lions' mouths opened in silent roars, the giraffes' necks stretched for the top of imaginary trees, the horses galloped majestically. The beasts were suspended from thick ropes attached to beams that protruded from a pole. Two burly and scruffy workmen rotated the pole. Children and adults sat atop the creatures, swinging and cheering as the workers sweated under the midday sun.

"Do you have a favorite?" his father asked.

Oskar nodded, breathlessly. "The horses."

Alexander put his arm around his son's shoulder. "Mine too."

"They're so beautiful," Oskar said. "Like they can fly."

"Do you want to ride it?" his mother asked.

Oskar shook his head. "I only want to watch."

The magical creatures circled. Calliope music played.

"Can you make a miniature version out of glass?" he asked his father.

Alexander laughed. "I don't think so. It would take a glass-blower with extraordinary skills. Skills straight from God."

"I bet you can. You can do anything." He pointed at the men, women, boys and girls who smiled and laughed as they rode the carousel. "People will feel like that when they see my glass sculptures." He turned to his parents, his expression thoughtful and serious. "Papa and Opa never went to school. Why do I have to?"

"Go ahead," Jana urged Alexander.

"Your *mutter* and I have decided if you make something out of glass on your own, you will not have to go back to school and I will teach you everything I know about glassblowing."

Tears flooded Oskar's eyes with such vigor it was hard to see. He gazed up at his parents and knew there were smiles on their blurred faces. He laughed, and then laughed more, so infectious his parents laughed and the people around them smiled and laughed too. He wiped his tears away and looked back at the horses and knew he would see them again.

The following morning, Oskar dressed and slowly walked behind the family home to the large, square shed used as a glassblowing studio where his father blew dishes, vases, pitchers, knick-knacks, and almost anything else requested and paid for by commoners, clergy, aristocrats and royalty.

"Don't come back until you're done," his father called.

Until this moment, Oskar had never lit the furnace, gathered the gather, or twirled the blowpipe on his own.

His parents' actions were calculated. Opa had done the same to Alexander, as had Opa's father before him. Alexander and Jana hoped to discover what comprised the soul of their son. Oskar hoped to master the riddles of the glass and the mysteries faced by glassblowers for the last 2000 years.

On a large wooden and aged worktable, three large bowls of silica sand, soda ash and lime greeted him. He looped a facemask around his nose and mouth and plastic glasses over his eyes, mixed the three substances and poured the combination into an iron crucible about one metre high and half as wide in diameter. A handle on top of the crucible's lid was thick enough to be grabbed with iron tongs.

He lit the wood under the furnace and waited. When it reached a raging temperature, he slipped on leather gloves and, using tongs, placed the container in the fire. He picked up a blowpipe and waited for the substance to liquefy. He had a short window to get this right. As he waited, he pictured what he hoped to create. A vase so beautiful and so fine his mother would run to church and thank God. His father would begin his apprenticeship in earnest and Oskar would never have to return to school.

The mixture liquefied. He removed the crucible with the tongs and placed it on a pile of bricks. He took the lid off and dunked the blowpipe into the clear, molten liquid. The heat on his face smothered him like a welcomed hug. He removed the pipe and spun it quickly, and then blew into the tube. Gravity turned the molten glass into the hourglass-shaped curves of a woman. With his free hand, he took a metal clamp and shaped the lip and neck of the forming vase, careful to work quickly and precisely. Spinning the tube again, he shaped the vase, feeling confident his parents would be proud of him and he would never be bullied again.

"I am going to be the best glassblower, not just in Austria but in the entire world," he declared.

He placed the vase on the worktable, stepped back and admired his work. In a moment, he would set the vase in the annealer to cool. He gasped as a crack formed at the lip of the vase, travelled down to the neck, over the shoulder and body and to the foot. His perfect vase split in two.

Chapter Nine

Father Mattheus sat in a pew and bent over the Book of the Departed. He had never written this much about a deceased member of his parish but Countess Anna was the exception to everything.

After Anna had died and he had convinced Franz to let him bless her body, he had *only* taken a quick peek at her breasts. He didn't touch them, merely snapped a photo with his mind. Not nearly as bad as what he assumed Franz was doing with her body.

He hadn't contacted the authorities after Franz battered James and stole Anna's body. What was the point? Franz and his family owned the people of power in Gloggnitz and the surrounding area. Besides, if he involved anyone of import, the investigation might turn from Franz to himself.

He read what he had written in the Book.

A noble creature. Excelled at knitting and archery. Loved horses, especially the Lipizzaners. Charitable. My beautiful love. Cause of death: Acute Putrid Fever. Oskar.

Oskar. The last word she said before she passed.

It couldn't be Oskar, nee Oskarina, that freak. Born a girl with all the body parts but pretended to be a man. His wife, Hedwig, going along with it. When Alexander and Jana Glasman joined his church thirteen years ago and met with him privately, he had done his job well. On the outside, he nodded appropriately, read passages from the Bible about accepting everyone for who they are, overlooked the negative passages on man having sexual relations with man, and explained that God makes no mistakes. On the inside, disgust rose in his throat like backwash from ingesting rotted meat. He wanted to love everyone, to accept all for who they are, but this he could not get past. It wasn't the sex part; he didn't care who had sex with whom. Mate with a beast for all he cared. It was the charade that Oskar embodied that disgusted him. At least Mattheus was honest about himself, a priest whose mind and heart filled with contemptuous thoughts and feelings that could only be purged with lashes, a man who longed for the peace of the afterlife.

After that first session with Alexander and Jana, Mattheus punished himself for his impure thoughts. That hadn't been his first time, the first occurred when he was a boy of six and living at the convent. He had placed the palm of his right hand over a flame, only to remove it when the smell of burning flesh reached his nostrils. He had found solace and healing in the self-inflicted punishment.

With the Book of the Departed heavy in his lap, he looked at his hand. The skin on his palm was still discolored, a lighter patch in the shape of a sickle.

Alexander and Jana had perished in a horse and carriage accident five years ago. Oskar and Hedy continued to attend Sunday services and, in fact, Oskar was very helpful. He lived a few doors down from the church, and only yesterday had assisted in carrying James to the doctor. But still, saying *he* instead of *she*, inviting Oskar to the events for men and not for women, a woman who pretended to be a man married to a woman who pretended to be married to a man, it was too weird for this pastor. He thought back to their wedding and how Mattheus maintained the façade of gaiety and approval.

The lashing he had administered to himself after the service ended was epic.

But if Oskar was *that* Oskar, the one whose name floated from Anna's lips, might he have to tell the freak's secret? Surely Oskar had manipulated her into believing he was more important than her loving pastor. Mustn't he be punished?

Mattheus eyed the handle of the whip that peeked from its hiding place under the pew. "No," he spoke aloud. "I have told no one the truth as I promised his parents. If I do, Oskar would surely be arrested and hanged. He's a good lad and doesn't deserve that. I mean, she's a good lass."

Anna's last spoken word was one mystery he might never solve unless he asked Oskar directly. Did he really want to know? He sighed and turned his attention back to the Book. *Cause of death: Acute Putrid Fever.* Putrid, indeed. Her body had burned with fever the days before her death. Her smell wedged in his nostrils as if glued. He had witnessed many die under these conditions. Once the skin began to flare and decay, there were no cures. It happened the same way each time. The head ached, the body chilled, and then the back, arms and legs cramped. Next, the fever came, high and for about three days. When it subsided, the person regained consciousness, spoke and desired food. Family and friends thanked God for the healing miracle, but within a couple of hours the fever and delirium returned. Soon, as the body rotted from inside out, the whites of the eyes and skin turned yellow. Vomiting commenced. Black blood shot up from the stomach and out through the nose and mouth. The only relief came from the cocoa plant. The relief was not for the dying as they were unconscious at this point, but was for the family and friends whose agony of watching their loved ones writhe in pain could only be eased by cocaine.

He wanted to blame Franz for her demise and to punish him for not taking better care of her. He wanted to reveal to the world the Count had extracted her blood for experiments. Who knew what else that maniac had done to her in his lab?

Many knew of his lab. While Manfred was a loyal servant, he also fancied the ladies and—when inebriated by alcohol and sex—told many secrets of the von Walsegg family and Stuppach Castle. For this reason, Mattheus stayed close with the prostitutes. He called them his Lady Network of Whores since they would pass secrets to him they had learned from important and drunk men. In exchange, Mattheus would help them skirt laws and would absolve them of their sins so they could go to heaven. This was how Mattheus knew much about the local government and members of his church. Who was sleeping with whom that wasn't his wife, what landowners treated farmers as serfs despite Joseph II's proclamation against this, and which parents refused to send their children to school even though doing so had become law.

Mattheus put quill to paper and wrote in the Book of the Departed.

Countess Anna von Walsegg was the loveliest of creatures. There are no words to sufficiently describe this being. Angelic comes close but is not sufficient. Her husband, Count Franz von Walsegg, is a sick man in his head. He has drawn blood from her for experiments. He dug up her body from its crypt and took her back to Stuppach Castle. His last words before running off with her like some primordial beast was that he wanted her to live forever. As I write this, I, Pastor Mattheus Richter, do not know what he is doing with her body but I know whatever it might be, it is sure to be a violation before God.

He stopped writing and reached into the pocket of his robe and withdrew a small silk satchel. The rose-colored bag fit in the palm of his hand and opened and closed by pulling and loosening a string woven into the folds of the fabric. He reached the thumb and forefinger of his right hand in and took the object out. The smell was so horrific he covered his mouth with the sleeve of his frock. Still, he was fascinated by what he held. It was smaller than when he first got it. It had shriveled and its hue had changed from a pinkish-beige to a greenish-purple. In a few days, it would be black, the nail would fall off, and eventually the skin would dry out and fall off too. All that would be left would be the phalanges.

He removed the sleeve from his nose and mouth and found the odor of the decaying finger mildly tolerable. He shook the bag and her wedding ring dropped into his palm. He slipped it onto his pinkie finger. He had gotten so fat over the years that it fit snugly. He brought her finger to his lips and kissed the tip and the knuckle. He rubbed the finger along his cheek.

"Oh, Mattheus, I adore you," he said. His voice octaves higher as he mimicked Anna's timbre. "Will you marry me?"

In his own voice, he responded, "I do."

He had no regrets severing Anna's finger. He deserved to have a part of her. He smiled at how clever he had been choosing her left ring finger. The finger where it was believed blood traveled directly to the heart. He wished he had more of her and felt a tinge of envy Franz had beaten him to the desecration of her crypt and the snatching of her body.

Mattheus reached under the pew and gripped the handle of the whip.

Chapter Ten

Oskar struggled to keep up with Raimund as they trudged through ankle high snow. The extra weight of his breasts slowed him. If Hedy didn't like them as much as she did, he would have cut them off a long time ago. It could be done, couldn't it? People lost arms and legs in battle and survived. Why couldn't the same happen with breasts?

He pulled his coat closer around him and pointed his chin down to avoid the sleet that drove into his face. At least the binding around his chest kept him warm. He hated leaving Hedy in such atrocious weather. It's not that she couldn't stoke the fire and keep warm; it was that he enjoyed providing the warmth for her.

Up ahead, the spires and long windows of Stuppach Castle glistened, so beautiful covered in snow like in a fairy tale. He wished he and Hedy could have children so he could sit them on his lap and tell them stories, but their body parts were all wrong. He pushed the regrets from his mind, no time for misgivings, only time to trudge forward.

What does Count Franz want from me now? Another crystal chandelier? A vase for a centerpiece for an official dinner? Could he want him to make a memorial for Anna?

Last time the Count had sent a messenger for him, he requested a real-sized glass violin, accurate down to the strings. That had been a difficult project but one Oskar enjoyed and conquered. The glass violin was displayed in Franz's music room. Others had asked Oskar to make one but he had refused as he had promised he would make only one. He knew not to cross the Count.

There was no mystery surrounding the Count's capabilities. Slayed a horse in the middle of a parade because the mare moved too slow, whipped a servant when she failed to avert her eyes from his, bloodied the girls and women he lay.

Oskar followed Raimund along the pathway. His toes numbed from the cold. Finally at the castle door, Manfred met them. A gold key hung on a chain around his neck. Oskar was happy to step into the warmth. The valet took his coat and led him toward the back of the castle. Raimund disappeared.

In a small hallway off the library, Manfred angled the key into a lock and opened a door.

Oskar peered in and hesitated at the sight of darkness. "Where is Count von Walsegg?"

"Down there."

He had heard about the secret lab in the castle and now knew it was true.

"It's dark," Oskar said.

"One moment." Manfred stepped into the library and returned holding a gold candelabra with a white taper candle. A gentle orange flame shimmered. He handed it to Oskar. "There are forty-one steps down." He pushed him forward.

The clank of the closed door and the grind of the lock startled Oskar. The light of the candle offered slight guidance. He took small steps forward, and felt the stone walls with his hands for guidance. He searched for the first step with his feet. There, found it. He stepped down. The candle lit one step at a time and cast eerie triangular shadows on the walls.

Oskar counted out-loud. *"Eins, zwei, drei."*

At the bottom, the large room was well lit by many candles that made the taper he carried insignificant. He blew it out. Count Franz stood before him wearing a surgical gown and gloves. He was covered with blood. There was a metal table also soaked with blood and overflowed with other chunky matter. Against a wall, an icebox and shelves with surgical tools loomed. The room reeked of a harsh stench Oskar had never smelled but recognized immediately as there was only one thing it could be. Death.

"Thank you for coming." The Count bowed as if bedecked in dinner tails.

Oskar forced a cordial nod.

"You know my dear Anna passed two days ago."

"Yes, I am sorry."

"You are to create the perfect memorial for her."

Oskar's heart leaped and he recalled her lavender smell, the lightness about her, and the dizzying affect she had on him. What memorial could befit a woman such as the Countess? Because of her love for the Lipizzaners, a horse was obvious, but Oskar had wanted to make that for her alone and not at the Count's command.

"It would be my honor to create a memorial for Countess Anna. Perhaps a glass bird."

"Not a bird."

"A flower then?"

"Not a flower."

"Then what?"

Franz stepped toward him. "My wife loved horses."

Oskar forced himself not to retreat. "I think I recall that."

"I would like you to make something with horses."

"Yes, sire. I will use the finest sand and mix it with— "

"No," the Count bellowed.

Oskar took a step back. "No?"

"You will not make it using standard ingredients. My Anna was anything but typical."

"What shall I use then?"

"I have the components here."

"You do?" Excitement tingled at his nerve endings. The Count was a very rich man. Had he cultivated the finest sand from the Sahara, the highest quality soda ash, and the perfect lime?

Franz opened the door to the cold box. Oskar stepped forward and looked in and then turned away. His stomach lurched and he regurgitated last evening's wiener schnitzel into the sink. He leaned over the edge and panted and gagged. Images of when he was thirteen years old soared through his mind. His father's voice was strong in his mind. Make something unusual out of glass today and you will not have to go back to school.

That first vase cracked down the middle. The second flopped over. The next one was too fat. The one after that fell onto its side. Oskar's tears flowed after each failure. Thoughts of having to return to school nauseated him. Whenever he threw up, that's what came to his mind. People making fun of him, laughing, locking him in closets. Twenty-one vases in all he had attempted before he came upon the perfect combination of heat, spinning, blowing through the long tube, and shaping the glass as it hardened. His mother brought him food and drink throughout the day and into the next morning.

When he showed his parents the twenty-second vase—fat bottomed with a long, sleek neck that flowered on top—his father put his arm around his shoulder and said, "Now it begins."

"What begins, Papa?" he asked.

"Your journey into the unusual."

He hadn't understood what he meant back then but as his apprenticeship progressed, he learned. This was a service-oriented profession, which meant the client was always right. His father taught him how to blow the traditional: beads for necklaces and bracelets, paperweights, tumblers, vases and ornaments. Throughout the years, he learned to make the atypical too: six-foot high glass flowers to adorn gardens, abstract sculptures, water pipes to smoke hashish and cannabis, and even a ten-inch penis for a concert pianist to place on his piano as he played.

Oskar considered himself an artist and enjoyed the challenges of different projects but...? He pushed himself off the sink, wiped his mouth with the back of his hand, and dared to peer into the icebox again.

"You want me to make glass from this?"

"Can you do it?" the Count's voice was urgent.

Could I make something from body parts? The thought was grotesque yet intriguing. The journey into the unusual, indeed. But this was Anna. Could he work with her desecrated body? Oskar looked back in the cold box, at the cleaned and stacked bones, at the glass jars filled with Anna's blood, and at her ground organs.

What would Anna think of her husband's request? Could he do it?

Chapter Eleven

It was a bright Sunday in June in 1778 and nine-year-old Oskar's first full day in Gloggnitz, he and his parents having moved from Vienna to leave Oskarina behind. At that time, the boy was pencil-shaped and favored knickers and a smart cap. His hair was cut short and he fancied the peach fuzz on his face to be the start of a beard. Life was full of promise.

Although the Glasmans arrived at their new home the evening before, exhausted and with much unpacking to do, they were up early and headed to church.

"The fastest way to get to know your neighbors is to pray with them," his father said.

Oskar took no issue. He was eager to meet new friends, the townspeople, his teachers, and his priest.

Gloggnitz was a lot smaller than Vienna, which pleased him. People walked along the dirt streets, three and four abreast, and smiled and waved. Women said *hallo* and men tipped their hats. Couples held hands. Parents swung their children in their arms and said *whoop-si-do* while the youngsters laughed. Fathers balanced young sons on their shoulders. Mothers warned their daughters not to allow their crinoline dresses to drag on the ground.

He strutted between his parents and his confidence grew. Oskar tipped his hat at passers-by.

"*Guten morgen,*" he said. "*Mein name ist Oskar.*"

*

At eight years old, Anna liked being a Flammbergin. The family derived riches from banking and trade and the clan was most admired for their beautiful singing voices. Wilhelm, Anna's father, conducted the church choir.

While they weren't the most admired family in town as that title belonged to the von Walseggs, they were held in high esteem.

"We breathe the same as those less fortunate," her father said. "We eat the same too. While you have all the comforts you need, one day you might not."

With those words, Anna became empathetic.

While the von Flammbergins weren't the wealthiest in town, that title too belonged to the von Walseggs, they never wanted for anything.

"Here." Her father bent on one knee and handed little Anna an Austrian florin. "Spend wisely. One day you could have nothing."

With those words, Anna became frugal.

"Treat everyone the same," her parents told her. "Regardless of their family history. Judge everyone by one thing."

"What is that?" she asked.

"By the level of their kindness."

With that, Anna became ideal.

*

The boy who sat in the church pew in front of her removed his cap. He must be new to town, Anna thought. He had pretty blond hair, soft and straight like a girl's yet cut short. Wisps of hair curled on the back of his neck. He recited verses with force and sang the hymns in a sweet mezzo-soprano unique for a boy. Anna found herself competing with him, to sing more vociferously and with sweeter tones. Soon, the two were so loud those around them stopped singing until the timbres of Anna and this new boy were the only voices that filled the pews. When they realized their vigor had funneled all the attention their way, they stopped singing. Anna's face turned red with embarrassment. The hair on the back of the boy's neck stood on end.

The church goers exploded with applause.

Father Mattheus banged a Bible against the pulpit. "*Schweigen.*" Silence.

The boy turned around and Anna's eyes met his. They smiled and knew they would be forever friends.

Chapter Twelve

At home, Oskar added a log to the wood-burning stove. Through belting snow and harsh winds, Raimund and Simon moved jars and cases from Stuppach Castle to the glassblower's studio.

Oskar stirred the cinders in the fire and wondered, *Can I make glass from Anna's body?* He knew he had to discuss this with Hedy, but how to bring it up?

"Come back to earth," Hedy said.

"I'm sorry. I was just thinking...whenever the Count asks us to do something, it ends up being trouble. I made a glass Madonna for him as a gift from him to Anna and he gave it to one of the women at the brothel. That last concerto you wrote he claimed as his own."

"That's okay. It wasn't very good. Wolfgang said it had promise but still— "

"That's not the point. Now, he wants me to make something using—"

"He's your best benefactor. You're not just making cups and plates for him. The violin you made was incredible. He might be crazy but his projects allow you to test your creativity *and* pay our expenses. Isn't that what you always say? You want to support us as an artist, not as the creator of common things you can purchase from any merchant?"

Hedy was right. He hadn't thought he could accomplish many of the Count's requests, but through the Count's odd demands he has could pursue glassblowing as an art form.

"I don't think there isn't anything you can't make from glass." Hedy wrapped her arms around his neck. "I bet you could build a castle of glass if you put your mind to it."

"You are my biggest fan, my love. The Count's latest assignment may prove too challenging."

"The memorial to Countess Anna. It seems to me that would be your honor. The horse that you blew was beautiful, and it was only a test. I know the final product will be spectacular, good enough to be displayed for all of eternity. She would be so proud, especially coming from you."

"It's not that simple. He wants me to make the memorial *out* of Anna."

Hedy smoothed back his hair. "You mean out of something that belonged to her?"

"No, I mean out of *her*."

"I don't understand."

"From her body."

Anna's hands dropped to her sides. She took a sideways step as if dizzy. Oskar steadied her with his hands on her shoulders.

"Is that why he took her from the crypt?" Her words were slow, stilted.

Oskar nodded. "The Count wants me to make something so she will live forever."

"Does Father Mattheus know?"

"I don't think anyone knows but me, and now you."

"You can't, Oskar. That must be sacrilegious or illegal or immoral, or all three."

He looked away. The brilliant orange and red embers in the stove warmed his face. "I shouldn't have told you. I should have protected you from this."

"We can't have secrets. Are you going to do it?"

He stuck his hand into his vest pocket and opened his palm toward Hedy.

Her eyes widened. "Fifteen ducats?"

"He will pay another twenty upon completion."

"That's more than you make in a year."

"Do you think Anna would think less of me if I do it?" he asked.

"I believe a lot of people make sacrifices in the name of art. I know Wolfgang has."

Oskar looked toward the front door. Anna would be arriving soon.

Chapter Thirteen
The Maestro's Home
Vienna, Austria

Mozart Wolfgang Amadeus despised wearing the heavy rug that draped over his scalp, around his ears and down his back. It had been okay when he was younger, when he cared about the latest fashions, the most popular headpieces, and the finest waistcoats. Now, at thirty-five years of age, with joint pain and shortness of breath, he had no tolerance for inconvenience. Not from people who were impossible to please, not from itchy clothing, and certainly not from burdensome wigs. He dabbed a handkerchief to his nose. The bleeding had stopped. The thrice daily nose bleeds were such a bore.

He removed the wig, flung it across the room and bent over the harpsichord once more. *The Magic Flute,* an opera in two acts, was almost complete. A *singspiel*, it combined music with spoken word. He cursed himself. *Why had I given a sample to Franz von Walsegg, that known pilferer of musical compositions?* Mozart had to finish the opera soon and claim it as his own before Franz von Wal-theif stole again!

To date, Mozart had composed over 600 works: symphonies, violin and piano concertos, masses, string quartets and sonatas. He believed *The Magic Flute* to be his final act. With the way his body was deteriorating and the fatigue he battled daily as onerous as the critics who thrived to condemn him, he was certain he did not have long to live.

With the balls of his thick fingers on the keys, he thought of his father Leopold, dead four years, and of his mother who had passed in 1778. He hadn't corresponded with his sister in three years. He mused upon the joys and hardships of life, the permanence of death, of how his hometown of Salzburg rejected him when he moved to Vienna over ten years earlier, and of his wife, Constanze, always pushing him to compose and unsympathetic when he complained of his swollen fingers and distended belly.

He would seize the day, as he's always done. He would put all these feelings—the regrets, the melancholy, the despondency, the raptures—into *The Magic Flute*. And then, perhaps, he would live forever.

Night exchanged places with the day. The bell-like sounds of a *glockenspiel* rang in his ears. Constanze would be home soon and would interrupt his creative process with complaints about what someone said about him at the market or how the press mischaracterized a statement or an aria of his. She would interrogate him on his progress and chastise him if she was dissatisfied.

"I am an old man." He would attempt to counter her discontent.

"You are only thirty-five."

"Correction. I am a young man in an old body."

To that, she would have no response.

A knock on the door and he lost his thoughts on Papageno, the funny bird-catcher in *The Magic Flute*. Constanze never knocked. *Who could it be?*

"Go away," he grumbled.

Silence, then three sharp raps again.

"Dammit."

He rose. His hips, knees and ankles groused. He made his way toward the door, hating that he shuffled like a man twice his age.

"Who is it?"

More knocks.

"Go away."

"I come with an important delivery." A voice seeped through the wood door, sounding comically masculine as if an attempt at a disguise. Was that Papageno's voice?

"Leave it on the floor and be gone."

"I cannot do that, *Herr* Mozart. My instructions are to deliver this letter directly to you."

He smiled. Yes, it was Papageno's voice. He would keep that voice in his mind as he composed. One never knew from where inspiration arose.

He flung the door open, hoping to catch the trickster in mid-knock. The front stoop was dark. The flame of the normally lit lantern above the door had been extinguished. Before him stood a person dressed in dark gray from shoes to winter cover to top hat. The stranger's chin tilted into his chest. Mozart studied *it* closely. *Was he really a she in disguise? Was he wearing a mask? Was he here to rob me? Or murder me? Would The Magic Flute never be finished?*

"Who are you?"

The dark stranger put his hand in his winter coat and withdrew quickly. Mozart flinched. Surely a dagger would be between his fingers. But he, or she, gripped not something hard and shiny, but flexible and made of paper. An envelope.

Mozart snatched it. "Who sent you?"

The gray messenger turned and was gone.

Chapter Fourteen
The Glassblower's Workshop
Gloggnitz, Austria
February 17, 1791

Like a carousel, Oskar rotated and took in the many containers. What was he to do with the jars of ground up bones, compressed skin, organs and blood? The studio smelled of death, yet if he concentrated he could discern the drops of lavender oil Anna dabbed behind her ears and inside her wrists. Still, he felt listless like a sagging newly-blown vase.

He sat at the thick wooden worktable and thought of all Anna had been, seeking energy with thoughts of her soothing voice, imagining the soft tips of her fingers brush his face, and seeing the wisps of hair on her arms move in a light breeze. He thought of her eyes, the path to her soul. Eyes that revealed her truth unmasked his. Looking into Anna's eyes, he had always felt she had the power to make dreams come true. She certainly had made one of his dreams come true. He had always wanted a friend who loved him unconditionally. Anna was that friend.

Other than Hedy, Anna had been his only friend and one of three living people who knew his secret. Pastor Mattheus knew but certainly wasn't a friend. He was his spiritual leader and Oskar readily helped when summoned by the priest, but that was the extent of their relationship. No socializing outside of the pews.

Oskar didn't dare get close to anyone else for fear he or she might learn his secret, and then what would be the result? He shuddered, knowing his true gender identity could be easily revealed. His voice, which he had labored to emit a full octave lower than Oskarina's, still at times came out higher if he was excited or scared. And what if a friend wanted to pat him on the back while they shared a stein, or gave him a friendly hug during a game of football, or while they played rugby he was tackled and his binding came loose?

Trapped between two worlds made forming friendships difficult. He wasn't queer since he was simply born in the wrong gender. He was a man who loved a woman. Yet he wasn't traditional either as he was a man with breasts and a vagina who loved a woman. Oskar sighed at the complicated and convoluted thoughts that always wracked his brain when he tried to identify who he was. He prayed one day he would be all Oskar with Oskarina gone forever. No more lilts in his voice, no more sex organs. He'd walk the streets of Gloggnitz as a man without binding and without having to place a stocking stuffed with cloth in his drawers to act as his bulge. Until that happened, he'd keep to himself and live as quiet of a life as possible, a life filled with Hedy and glasswork.

He thought of one of his last conversations with Anna before she grew ill. Hedy had been in Vienna for the day visiting Wolfgang and Anna had paid Oskar a lovely surprise visit. She had told the Count she was training an unruly Lipizzaner and would be home late.

"I want to be a man." It was not the first time he had shared this with Anna.

"You are a man," Anna replied. "In your heart, that's who you are."

"Is it wrong of me to want more?" He looked down at his chest. "Or less?"

"Don't be foolish."

"There has to be a skilled surgeon to remove these things. They're mistakes, like tumors. Aren't tumors meant to be removed? Perhaps Dr. Artz could do it."

"They are breasts, Oskar, and they are yours to keep."

"They were meant for another. I know it."

"You are speaking like a madman."

"Perhaps, but I'd rather be a mad man than a sad woman."

Oskar smiled at the memory. How many times had he expressed this desire to Anna, the desire to really be a man? He rarely spoke to Hedy about it; she shushed him immediately and he hated to make her upset. But Anna listened, and then always reached the same conclusion. Surgery was too risky. Oskar had to learn to be happy with who he was, and no longer concentrate on who he wasn't.

In the studio, he took out paper and a charcoal pencil and sketched a horse. A Lipizzaner reared back on its haunches with his front legs in the air as if about to take flight. Oskar admired the drawing. It was a good first composite but the Count had wanted more than one horse to memorialize the Countess. Oskar thought how best to do that. How to create something beautiful and lyrical all at once, a work of art that would be delicate yet would stand the test of time, that could survive the direst of events and be admired for all of eternity? It not only had to be strong and sturdy, yet also of such a design that no matter the trends in art, Anna's memorial would remain something to be exhibited and admired. A piece that could live its life in a museum long after Oskar was gone.

He drew more horses, prancing and leaping, strongly muscled, necks thrown back with glee. An Arabian, a Palomino, a Bay, an Appaloosa. For fun, he gave them wings. He leaned back, pleased. Yes, he could blow these horses from glass. With the detail he envisioned it would take practice but he was sure he could get them right. But then, what to do with them? How to make them fly?

He flashed back to the day his parents had taken him to a carnival, the day they had told him he could be a glassblower and not have to return to school, the day he marveled at the first carousel he had ever seen.

"Can they fly?" he remembered asking his father.

"Not literally, son," Papa had said, "but if you listen to the music and close your eyes I bet you can see them take flight."

Oskar did just that and his father had been correct. As they circled, he closed his eyes and saw the horses soar into the pale blue sky, high over Vienna where they glided along the Danube.

Oskar opened his eyes. "I bet you can make that out of glass."

His father laughed. "I don't think so but it sure would be fun to try."

Oskar was ready to try. He'd make four of the most magnificent creatures ever to grace a carousel. Bedecked in jewels, he'd place them on a glass platform and rig it so it moved like a life-sized carousel. Music would play. Countess Anna von Walsegg would live forever and, perhaps, one day Oskar would join her.

He saw the containers and glass jars on the studio shelves and his heart drooped. Fantasy was one thing, but this reality was another. He wished his father was still alive and they could do this together yet, Oskar wondered, would he work with me on it, or would he tell me it was sacrilegious and I would go to hell?

"Perhaps I should speak with Father Mattheus before I begin?" he said out loud.

"What about Father Mattheus?" Hedy stood at the door to the glassblowing studio.

"My love." He beamed.

She stepped in. "Let me see."

He held up the newly blown horse.

"Is it made from...Anna?"

He shook his head.

Hedy studied the horse, bent in close but did not touch.

"I have to get it in the annealer." He slipped his hands into gloves and transferred the glass horse from the workbench into the cooling oven. He took off the gloves and turned to his wife.

"Why are you crying?"

"It's so beautiful. You are the best glassblower in all of the world."

"Oh, Hedy. To love me so unconditionally, that is the greatest gift of my life."

He leaned in and their lips met softly, and then parted for their tongues to explore.

Oskar loved everything about her, her smell, her taste, the softness of her skin. He untied the string on her cloak and pushed it off her shoulders. She wore a simple housedress she had made herself. She turned, her back to him, and he un-buttoned the back of her dress.

He took his time, each button delicate between his finger-tips, enjoying as Hedy's freckled back was slowly exposed. With each button that became undone, he kissed the bare skin that was revealed, all the way down to her hips until he was on his knees. He put his hands under her dress and enjoyed the warm feel of the skin on her thighs. He stood and she faced him. He gently removed the dress from her shoulders and it fell to the floor.

She stepped out of it, a stunning vision as she slipped off her panties. She wasn't wearing a bra. She never needed one.

She rubbed her body against his and his hands felt all of her. Her buttocks, the small of her back, the curve of her hips, her shoulder blades, the tops of her arms, her elbows, and down to her thighs, knees and calves. On his knees again, with his stunning wife before him, he tasted her. Slow at first, then faster as his hunger increased and a stirring in his own loins built. He stood and lifted her. She locked her legs around his midsection and he carried her to the workbench where he placed her down gently. They kissed and he penetrated her with his fingers.

Her groans were soft, like mews. He enjoyed knowing her verbal signs, her physical signs too. How she moved when she wanted it harder, when she was about to cum. Her hands ran up and down his back, along his arms, over his face. She reached for the buttons on his shirt.

Oskar grabbed her hands. "No," he said softly.

"I want you like you want me."

He sighed. This wasn't always a problem, but sometimes Hedy wasn't satisfied only receiving, she wanted to give too. He hated saying no, hated to deprive her of her desires, but to let her touch him—like that—meant he had to acknowledge who he was, who he wasn't.

"Please."

He nodded, a gentle nod accompanied by a pit in his stomach. *Let go*, he told himself, *even if it doesn't please me, it pleases her.*

He kissed her again. The excitement built inside of him and his fingers plunged deep into her. Hedy's contractions pumped against his fingers. Her sweet mouth in an O as he stayed close to her and felt her breath on the skin of his face. She fell into him, breathed heavily, only taking a moment's respite before unbuttoning his shirt and slipping it off. She jumped from the worktable and undid the binding around his chest, a gentle, erotic dance.

He closed his eyes as the binding fell to his feet. He didn't want to see his breasts, those large, ugly things that proclaimed all that was wrong with him. Because of his breasts, he couldn't please his wife like a real husband. Because of those *things*, he lived in fear. Hedy caressed them, in a way only a woman knew how to do. Soft groans rose from her mouth. She brought her mouth to his nipples, flicked one and then the other with her tongue.

A noise. From the front of the studio. A laugh, perhaps. Or a snicker. Count Franz von Walsegg stood in the open doorway. He held a glass bottle. Oskar quickly picked up his shirt and put it on, fumbled with the buttons, his breasts obvious under the thin fabric. Every muscle in his body tensed. His heart pounded with such force he was sure the rhythm could be heard all the way to Vienna.

The Count stepped into the studio. "I always thought there was something strange about you. It was your hands. They're big but delicate, like my grandmother's hands."

Hedy jumped in front of Oskar. "Leave him alone."

The Count laughed. "You're going to have your *wife* protect you?"

Oskar stepped in front of her. "Count Von Walsegg, please..."

Franz walked to him until they were a breath apart. He looked Oskar up and down, paused to stare at his breasts through the fabric, and touched his right breast. Oskar tensed, unsure what he should do. *Let him touch me? Slap his hand away? Punch him in the mouth? Kill him?*

Franz dropped his hand to his side. "We all have secrets, Oskar. You know one of mine." He held up the bottle with the yellow stones inside. "Now I know one of yours."

Oskar eyed a scoring knife on the worktable near him, careful to mark its location. If the Count touched Hedy, he would use it for sure.

Franz looked from Hedy to Oskar. "Perversion is so interesting, isn't it? You know what it means, right? Unacceptable or weird sexual behavior. Do you know what it also means? It's also changing something from what it was intended to be. You, Oskar Glasman, were born a girl and that is what you were intended to be but look at you and your sham."

"Please do not tell anyone. I beg you."

"And you, dear Hedy, do you find it easier to justify your love for women by pretending you are married to a man?"

"That is enough." Oskar grabbed the scoring knife. "It is one thing for you to dishonor me but it is unacceptable for you to dishonor my wife."

"Ah," Franz smiled, "you play the role of husband well. But tell me, how do you convince yourself daily you are a man with such large breasts?"

Oskar fought the tears to stay behind his eyes. "I wish more than anything to remove them."

Franz walked around the studio, looked at the kiln, the annealer, the vases, cups and other glass objects made by Oskar and Hedy. "Why is it you've never invited me to visit your studio?" He did not wait for an answer but turned to the shelves filled with Anna's remains. "I never understood what Anna saw in you."

"You knew of our friendship?"

"I knew it wasn't sexual. I was enough of a man to please my wife. But now, I understand. She always expressed tenderness for underdogs and freaks. Tell me, did she know the truth?"

Oskar nodded.

"She kept your secret well. Who else knows?"

"That's none of your business," Hedy said.

Franz laughed. "Maybe that was true one minute ago, but no longer."

"Father Mattheus," Oskar said. "No one else needs to know. We work hard. We bother no one. Please."

"What do you think would happen if your secret was revealed?"

Hedy went to the worktable and picked up a rod nipper. "You will do no such thing."

Oskar looked from Hedy to Franz, unsure what to do. He felt emasculated, his wife coming to his rescue, allowing the Count touch him without swatting his hands away, holding the scoring knife but doing nothing with it.

Oskar stepped forward. "Leave."

Franz held out the glass jar he carried. "These are Anna's teeth. They were left behind in the lab."

Oskar took the jar from him.

Franz turned. At the door, he looked back. "Come to the palace tomorrow, first thing in the morning. Both of you. Meet me in the lab."

"And if we do not show?" Hedy asked.

"I dare you to find out."

Chapter Fifteen

The lab felt bleaker than the last time he was there a couple of days earlier. It was hard to believe all that had occurred since Anna's death four days ago. Her tomb dug up, her body dissected, the Count's desire to have her memorialized forever in glass, and then Oskar's worse nightmare come to life, his secret revealed.

The leather of the bottom of his boots gripped the stone stairs. With his hand firm around Hedy's waist, he guided her into the dark well. He counted forty-one steps. He had tried to talk her into staying behind by saying he would handle whatever craziness the Count had in mind, but there was no convincing his wife to not take this journey with him into the abyss.

All night long they had discussed the possibilities of what the Count wanted. Perhaps, they theorized, he would threaten to reveal Oskar's secret unless Oskar did something for the Count, maybe even involve Hedy and try and take advantage of her relationship with Mozart. Or maybe the Count's desires were more perverse. In bed, with their arms around each other, shielding out the cold February chill that seeped through the stone walls of their home, neither disagreed when Hedy suggested the Count might be attracted to Oskar and his feminine body parts.

The sun began to soften the horizon. Oskar snuggled into his wife, enjoying her warmth, her sweet smell, and her sleepy breath on his neck.

"You're not going," he said.

She sat up. "Oskar Rupert Glasman, I am going and that is final."

Oskar tried to hide his smile but couldn't. She only called him by his full name when she was angry with him, something she never pulled off well. Hedy giggled and the two broke into laughter, at first from their bellies but then catching in their throats as giddiness and fear collided. Oskar closed his eyes and buried his head in her chest. He would talk her in to staying home after their morning sponge baths.

Morning bloomed and his pleas shot into the air and fell stale onto the hard floor. Bundled against a driving, bitter wind, they made their way by foot to Stuppach Castle. Clutching each other, neither spoke.

Hedy hesitated on a step that led down into the lab and Oskar tightened his grip around her waist. At the bottom of the stairs, a triangular yellow beam of light rested on the stone floor. Oskar moved into the light and looked into the lab. Standing behind the wooden table was Count von Walsegg who was bedecked in a knee-length lab coat. The left side of his face was lit by flickering candles arranged on a small side table. The right side of his face was as dark as the devil. The candles circled surgical tools and cast their elongated dancing shadows against a wall.

"Welcome." The Count bowed as if he had invited them to tea.

Oskar stepped forward and positioned Hedy behind him. "We're here. What do you want?"

The Count snickered. "Patience, Oskar, or should I call you Oskarina?"

The pit in Oskar's stomach sank deeper than he had imagined it could ever go. "We shouldn't have come." Oskar was surprised to hear his thought emit into words.

The Count walked toward them. The heels of his thick leather boots clicked on the floor. He neared Oskar and ran his index finger along his cheek.

Oskar swatted his hand away.

"What is it you want?" Hedy asked. "We came only because you threatened to reveal Oskar's secret if we didn't. Tell us what you want."

The Count pointed at Oskar and laughed. "And he's the man of the family?"

"That's it," Oskar said. "Let's go."

"Leave and all of Gloggnitz will titter with the news of the he-she by suppertime. And then what? Will you be able to outrun the men who will fuck you and kill you? Or maybe they'll kill you first."

"How dare you!" Hedy said.

"You are a curiosity, Oskar. Female body parts and the face and mannerisms of a male. I have a mind to fuck you myself. I've always wanted to fuck your wife but now you are more tantalizing to me. But that is not why I asked you here."

"Tell us why?" Oskar demanded.

"To barter."

"I have nothing to offer other than my skills as a glass-blower."

"There is something *you* want that I can provide. There is something *I* want you can give me. Isn't that the requisite foreplay before any erotic arrangement?"

"What is it you want?" Hedy snapped.

"I want to practice my skills as a surgeon."

"You have no training," Hedy said.

"I do in my own lab." He waved an arm, the ringleader of his circus. "Here, I am whoever I desire to be."

"How can I help you practice your skills as a surgeon? You already dissected Anna. What more do you want?"

The Count looked at Oskar's chest, his breasts expertly bound by Hedy that morning.

Oskar took a step back. "No."

"Isn't that what you desire? To be a true man?"

"Yes, of course, but not under your scalpel."

"Suit yourself," the Count said. "There is a church service this afternoon. I will announce your fraud before the congregation."

"Wait," Oskar said.

"You're not considering this." Hedy grabbed his arm.

"No. Yes. I don't know. Can't we barter for something else? I want nothing more than to have these atrocities removed but not under your knife. What's the point if I bleed to death on your operating table?"

"That's a risk you'll have to take. Consider your choices. A sure death when I tell everyone or you can put your faith in these." He held up his hands and wiggled his fingers.

"How about if we find a proper surgeon and allow you to watch? We can go to Vienna, or Dr. Artz can do it." Hedy said.

"No. Me. Here. In my lab. That is my only offer."

"Never." Hedy spat.

Oskar turned toward her. "Perhaps we should discuss it."

"Oskar Rupert Glasman, I will never allow this man to touch you again."

Oskar didn't laugh this time as Hedy admonished him by speaking his full name. She was right. He would never escape the Count's knife alive. If he didn't bleed out on his table, he would surely hobble home with an infection that would drain the life from his body slowly and painfully and leave him a sliver of the sliver of the man he used to be. But to tell the townspeople his secret would surely end in his demise.

What would happen to Hedy if his—if their—secret was revealed? He recoiled at the thought of any harm to her. He looked to the Count. Their eyes met in silent assent.

Chapter Sixteen

The cloaked hunched back figure at the front door to Hedy and Oskar's home swayed side-to-side. Hedy let go of Oskar's arm and ran to him. She wrapped her hands around his shoulders and steadied him. Oskar hurried and opened the door. Together, they helped Wolfgang settle in Oskar's chair in front of the wood burning stove. Mozart's valet, horse and carriage waited outside in the snow bound yard, warmed by the morning sun. Inside, the composer thawed.

Hedy made hot cider. Oskar stared at the composer's red and swollen hands.

"You are wondering how I play the piano and score music?"

"I am."

"They do not begin to swell until several hours after I wake. I compose first thing in the morning." He shifted his body more toward the heat of the stove.

Hedy walked in and carried a tray with three steaming mugs of cider. She put two down on a table between where Mozart and Oskar sat, and held one between her hands, warming them. She inhaled the sweet steam.

Mozart sipped the cider and licked sugar from his lips. "A gray messenger came to see me yesterday. He brought this." He reached into his cloak and pulled out a letter. He handed it to Oskar.

Oskar read aloud. "Dear Maestro, It is with great favour I request the indulgence of your flair in writing a Requiem

Mass. I acknoeledge I am looking ardently toward the completion of your work and will pay great sums. Please, kind sir, provide your acceptance, fee and delivery date to..." Oskar looked at Mozart. "It lists the name and address of an attorney for you to contact with your response."

"I've consulted with Constanze and sent a reply."

"What is it?" Hedy asked.

"I accepted the commission but without promise of a date of delivery."

"And...?"

"My valet dropped it off this morning. I told them I would await here until dusk for their response." Mozart looked into the air. "If my counteroffer is accepted, it will be my final requiem."

"Don't say that, Wolfgang." Hedy reached out for his hand.

"A man knows when he is going to die. I will not see 1792."

"That's not true."

Mozart brought the back of her hand to his lips. "Always the optimist, my dear, even when you were a small girl."

Hedy blushed. Oskar knew Mozart had that effect on her. The maestro and the student, she always looked up to him, defended him when people called him arrogant and egotistical, and loved him through his most difficult spells.

Mozart sputtered and coughed. A spattering of blood landed in his hankie, which he folded to hide the glob. He wiped his lips and took a slow sip of cider.

"I am positive they will be here soon with their acceptance," Hedy said.

"I am not as sure. The terms of my counteroffer may be unacceptable. No contract, no attorneys, no timetable, no cri-

ticism or comments. Those are the only terms of my acceptance."

Oskar rose and motioned for Hedy to sit. She accepted and
Oskar retrieved a stool from the kitchen and sat in front of
them in a trilogy of artistic genius.

Oskar leaned toward Wolfgang. "We are craftsmen. You
create through music. I create through glass. Our livelihood is
through accepting commissions."

"Yes, you are correct, my lad, but when you are sick and
dying you too will weigh the value of a wage versus the value of
the integrity of your work and the reputation you hope to leave
behind."

"Yes, I am sure I will. But I also appreciate that physical
and creative strength is fortified through food and shelter, as
well as through the hope I will be able to leave something last-
ing behind for those I love."

Mozart coughed again and brought the clean side of the
hankie to his lips. Hedy took a napkin and wiped a smidgen of
blood from the side of his mouth.

"Sometimes," Oskar continued, "we accept offers that come
with risks because we have no choice."

"Why is it we are often so good at resolving other people's
problems over our own?" Mozart mused.

"What do you mean, Wolfgang?" Hedy asked.

"It is clear you are both troubled. "

"Why do you think something is troubling us?" Oskar asked.

"Hedy's eyes are swollen from crying and your jaw is set
tighter than a virgin's twat."

"Wolfgang!" Hedy admonished.

"Forgive me. With age comes less filters." He held out his
mug. "A refill, dear?"

Hedy took the mug and went into the kitchen.

"Now," Mozart said, "man-to-man. Are you having marital problems? Have you taken a mistress?"

"No, no, nothing like that."

"Good, because I would kill you if you betrayed my Hedy. What then?"

Oskar studied Wolfgang, who had served as his surrogate father since he and Hedy married. But what would he say? How could he explain? Slowly, he reached for the buttons on his shirt. He knew of no better way to share his secret than to show it.

"What are you doing?" Hedy entered the sitting area, her fingers wrapped around a steaming mug of cider.

Oskar's hands froze. "I wish for guidance."

"I have given you all the guidance you need."

Oskar resumed unbuttoning his shirt.

"Don't," Hedy said. "You're not just revealing yourself but me too."

Oskar continued. His fingers slipped a button through a slit, and then moved to the one below. Tears filled his eyes. He didn't want to hurt her but felt desperate. He needed the advice of someone venerable. Who better than Wolfgang Amadeus Mozart, the man who could fix all problems with music?

Mozart coughed. A spasm of hacks incapacitated him. The hankie was soon covered in blood with no more folds to hide the spew.

He sipped the cider and looked from Oskar to Hedy. "What is it?"

"We have a secret," Oskar said.

"That will remain a secret," Hedy said. "Do not burden the maestro with our ailments. He is sick enough."

"Please, I would like another opinion." Oskar pleaded.

"Since when is your wife's opinion not good enough?" Hedy asked.

"I've accepted his offer." Oskar blurted. His shirt was half-open, the binding exposed.

"You what?" Hedy said.

"Enough," Mozart bellowed. He looked to Hedy. "Hedwig Melody Glasman. Talk. Now."

Hedy raced through the explanation of Oskarina becoming Oskar, of what happened in the studio when the Count walked in on them and of his demand they go to his lab. She explained his offer, and how she just learned Oskar accepted it. Mozart listened with closed eyes, hearing each note of Hedy's opus.

Mozart placed a shaking hand on Oskar's face. "As you said to me, Oskar Glasman, sometimes we accept offers that come with risks because we have no choice. But sometimes, my son, the risks are too great."

Chapter Seventeen

Wolfgang Amadeus Mozart

Salzburg, Austria

June 25, 1773

A symphony raged in seventeen-year-old Wolfgang Amadeus Mozart's brain. Alone and seated on a wooden bench inside his family's apartment, his back was curved and his long fingers were poised over a piano. Heat from the keyboard sucked into his pores. It was a pleasant twenty-three degrees centigrade outside. The windows were open and he enjoyed a crossbreeze. There was no need for a fan in the three-bedroom flat he shared with his parents and sister at 9 Getreidegasse, yet sweat soaked his white, blousy shirt. His long, dark curly hair plastered to the back of his neck and face. The music did this to him. Nothing else had, or would. No woman, no possession, no other emotion. He loved birthing an arrangement even if he was sure each new composition seized years from his life.

I will die young, he believed, but my music will live forever.

A melody continued to play in his mind. Fingers hovered over the upright as he waited for the moment when the sonata traveled from his consciousness through his veins and to the keyboard.

At the first scream, his back straightened and he wondered if the sound was imagined. With the second shriek, he knew the vibration was real. He jumped and knocked the bench askew.

"Kerstin." He ran to the apartment next door.

The door was unlocked as they had arranged. Deniz, Kerstin's husband, was at work. The baby wasn't supposed to arrive until the following week. Just in case, the Mozarts had promised to be available should the baby decide to appear off-schedule. Mozart hadn't considered the child would come when he was the only one home. He never considered much that didn't involve music.

He burst into her apartment. Kerstin was on the floor. Her long blonde hair splayed against her pale face. Her legs were opened under a damp housedress. She lay in a puddle of water.

"I'll get the wet nurse," he yelled.

"No time." She panted and pulled her dress back. "Help me, Wolfgang."

He dropped to the floor. His knees landed in her wet. Kerstin was wide open in front of him. He had never seen a woman down there. Wet, black curled hair grew in a mound and onto her inner thighs. She was dark and damp.

"He's coming. He's coming." She screamed. "Get a towel. A sheet."

Mozart ran to the bedroom and fisted everything on the bed, including a blanket, sheets, and pillows, and ran back to the living room. He slid to his knees and positioned himself in front of her spread legs. He stared at her wet, hairy mound and dared himself not to look away for fear the baby would shoot out and land headfirst on the hard floor. The opening widened. The smell of her sweat mixed with his. Kerstin's screams grew in tempo and volume. He positioned the blanket under her bottom. He took the sheet and wrapped it around his hands.

A mess of hair crept out and Kerstin wailed. Mozart's heart thudded like a bass drum. His analytical mind reasoned that millions of babies had been born since the time of cavemen. This is a natural process. All he had to do was wait and the baby would do the rest.

"Get him out of me," Kerstin cried.

"What? How?"

"Its head. Grab its head."

"I can't."

"Do it." Her scream was guttural, from a place Mozart hadn't yet learned existed.

He placed his hands on the baby's head and pulled. It didn't move.

"What do I do?"

"Aaaargh!" She screamed. "The baby. Help my baby."

Mozart positioned himself on his knees, one hand on each side of the baby's head. More forcefully, he pulled. *Please don't let me hurt him.* With the power of his hands, with his will, while Kerstin pushed and gasped, the head emerged, and then shoulders, a tiny torso, arms and legs. A mess of blood and fluids drained onto the blanket. The purple twisted umbilical cord followed.

Slowly, Kerstin raised her shoulders from the floor. She glistened with sweat. Her eyes grew wide. "Why isn't the baby crying? Oh my God, he's blue. Cut the umbilical cord."

"With what? How?"

"A knife. Hurry."

He ran to the kitchen and returned with a sharp blade.

"Tie it off," she ordered. "Cut it close to the baby."

He pulled a pillowcase off a pillow and tied it like a tourniquet around the slimy cord. He severed it with the kitchen knife and then found a clean part of the sheet and wiped the blood and muck from the motionless newborn.

"Why doesn't it cry?" he asked.

"Hit it." Kerstin said.

He tapped the baby on its belly.

"Hit it hard. Hurry. On its backside."

He turned the baby over and slapped it sharply on its bottom. Nothing.

"Do it again. Harder." Kerstin shrieked.

He struck the baby urgently with his open hand. A sharp pop sounded. A red mark formed on its buttocks.

And then, the most beautiful sound, a high frequency, a perfect tone, loud and strong. The baby wailed, its face the most beautiful shade of crimson.

Kerstin cried and lay back on the floor. "He's okay."

With the baby swaddled in the sheet and tears in Mozart's eyes, he handed the newborn to Kerstin. "Your baby boy is a girl."

Kerstin cuddled the newborn and laughed. "Deniz and I were so certain we were going to have a boy we never chose any girls' names. Oh, Wolfgang, you choose her name."

"Me?"

"Please. I can't think. I am so delirious with joy. She's beautiful and you saved her."

"Deniz will want to pick a name."

"When I tell him how brave you were and how you saved our baby's life, he'll want you to name her. I'm positive."

He gazed upon the newborn who buried her head in her mother's breasts and cooed. He had helped birth something more important than a composition. Euphoria pulsed through his body, elation, jubilation, joy.

"Her first name will be Hedwig because she is a fighter. Her middle name will be Melody because she is the most beautiful composition notes could ever form."

"Wonderful. We will call her Hedy for short."

He stroked the child's head, sticky from birth. "I promise you, Hedy Melody, you will never travel this world alone."

Chapter Eighteen

In the small room in the back of the rectory, Father Mattheus plowed a blade across his forearm. Blood oozed from the jagged line like a beautifully scripted homily. It had been four days since he pilfered Anna's final breath and three since Franz stole her from the crypt. He gently, yet deeply, pulled the blade across his forearm again, slash number two. What could Franz have done with her body? He had heard about methods to preserve birds, something sportsmen were doing to display their conquests. Had Franz discovered a way to stuff her body and mount her on a wall? He had also heard from his Lady Network of Whores that post-coitus Franz liked to talk about a laboratory he had built in Stuppach Castle. He already knew Franz had withdrawn blood from Anna, for what purpose he wasn't sure. Had Franz now taken this weird hobby to another, more sordid, level?

Pain boiled inside of him and Mattheus drew a third line across his arm, momentarily relieving his heartache in the drops of blood that dripped onto his frock and the straw bed. The smell of metal mixed with that of decay and dung. He dug his hand, the one that wasn't bloodied, into the straw and pulled out a small silk satchel. He loosened the string woven into the fabric and gagged when a putrid smell shot out like a flame. His eyes watered and he breathed through his mouth and tried to overcome the stench. He pushed the sleeve of his frock higher on his bicep and dug the blade into his arm, drawing a fourth and final line, one for each day since Anna was taken from him. This final cut deeper, most excruciating, and the loveliest of the quartet.

He removed the decomposed finger from the satchel and ran the tip along his cheekbone, down his chest, and along the hair that formed a line to his genitals.

"I am okay, my love," he said. "This pain I feel is nothing compared to losing you. It makes me feel better to suffer as you have." He placed her finger back in the satchel, tucked it into the straw bedding and raised the blade to his neck. "Perhaps I should join you, wherever your soul might be." He pressed the blade against his jugular. Its jagged edge dug into his loose skin. A prick of blood peeked into daylight.

"Wait." Mattheus' voice was high-pitched.

"What, my sweet?" He held the knife under his jowls.

"Don't join me yet." He spoke as Anna.

"Why do you make such a request?" He asked.

"You must put me back in my grave so we can be buried together."

"How do I find you? Where are you? Are you in his lab?" He lowered the bloodied knife to his lap. "Anna? Are you there?"

Blood covered his left arm and hand, dripped onto his frock, his bed. A wave of dizziness, then nausea, ballooned around him.

"Anna? Are you real?"

He grabbed a cloth from his side table and dapped at the cuts on his arm, wincing at the sharp stings.

"Anna? How do I find you? Send me a sign."

"Father," a voice called from the front of the rectory.

Mattheus quickly wrapped the cloth around his forearm and pulled his sleeve down. He jumped up and scurried to the front of the church. Anna had done it. She sent him a sign.

Chapter Nineteen

Mattheus was pleased when he stepped into the church from the back and saw it was Oskar, alone. Maybe now he could find out the meaning behind Anna's last word.

It amazed Mattheus how Oskar and Hedy looked like any other married couple who attended church on Sundays. If his parents hadn't confessed the truth about their daughter when they moved to Gloggnitz, the priest might never have figured it out. He had known Hedy and her family since she was young too, admiring her inner strength and athletic ability and secretly blessing her defiance of authority.

"Where is your lovely wife?" Mattheus pointed Oskar toward a pew.

He did not move. "I come to seek your advice, Father. I am here with her blessing as we have no secrets."

Mattheus' arm throbbed. He strived to hide any sign of pain from alighting his face. "What is it, my son?"

Oskar exhaled weightily. "You have accepted me, Father. I've wished my parents hadn't told you but now I am glad. You have held my secret well and for that I am eternally grateful."

Mattheus' knees buckled. The pain on his arm excruciating like a vulture trying to peck its way out of his skin. He grabbed the back of a pew.

Oskar reached for him. "Are you okay?"

"Yes, yes." Mattheus sat hard. "I'm afraid my gout is acting up."

"Shall we speak another time when you are not ailing?"

"Now is fine."

Oskar sat in the pew in front of him and twisted his body to face the preacher. "May I get you some water? You're sweating."

"You are not here to tend to me but for me to tend to you. What is it, my child?"

"Well, uh, well..."

"Speak without fear."

"You know my, um, situation." Oskar folded his arms across his chest. "I can no longer be only a man in my mind. Do you know what it's like to hold a secret? To be fearful you will be discovered and then...?"

"What?"

"The consequences."

"God loves us no matter what."

"If He loves me so much, why was I born female?"

"Just because God loves us doesn't mean He doesn't give us challenges."

"If this is a test, when do I learn if I pass or fail?"

"We all pass, my child."

Oskar sighed. "I shouldn't have come." He moved to leave.

Mattheus grabbed his arm. "Don't go. Tell me, what is on your mind?"

Oskar settled back into the bench and looked at Mattheus's hand. "You're bleeding."

"Oh, so I am." He wiped the blood with his other sleeve. "Seems I cut myself worse than I had thought when I was fixing the barn. James is still unable to return to the grounds since the Count seemed fit to beat him."

"If James isn't available, you should summon me."

"I should know better than to think this old, fat man can fix a leaky roof without being injured." He laughed weakly. "I will be fine. Continue."

"Someone has discovered my secret and means to tell all at Sunday's service, only two days from now, if I don't...You see, I so badly do not want these..." He motioned toward his breasts. "...He wants to remove them for me but he is no doctor. If I won't allow it, he will tell all the truth. I am afraid I won't survive the operation and what would happen to Hedy then? Or if he tells everyone I'm not a man, what will happen to me in that case, and Hedy too? I fear so much for her, Father."

"Slow down."

"I should have only loved her from afar. You introduced us, Father. Did you know we'd fall in love and we would marry? Why didn't you let me stay in my workshop, alone, where I could do no harm? You drew me out and I trusted you. I can't stand the thought of Hedy being hurt because of me." Oskar's eyes widened. "You married us, Father. What if the townspeople find out you knew all along? What might happen to you? I never thought living true to myself could cause so much trouble and so much risk to my wife. I've spent my entire life hurting people, haven't I? I disappointed my parents who wanted me to join a convent and live a studious life. They didn't want me to live the life of a glassblower, my hands burned, the whiskers on my face singed, indebted to the whim and whimsy of wealthy madmen."

"Stop," Mattheus yelled.

Oskar slumped and cried.

Mattheus waited, willed himself not to pass out from the pain while he calculated the best way to turn Oskar's misfortune into his own fortune.

"Who is this person who threatens to reveal your secret?"

Oskar hesitated. "The Count."

Mattheus quickly put the pieces together. The stories of Franz's underground lab were true. Bless you, my Lady Network of Whores. Who had Franz operated on? Would Oskar be the first? Or perhaps the first living patient? Mattheus now gleaned what might have happened to several servants over the last few years who, as the preacher was told, stopped coming to church since they allegedly had to leave town due to family emergencies. Had they never left? Would their remains be discovered in the fields behind Stuppach Castle?

"The Count found out about me," Oskar explained. "He says I must agree to let him remove my breasts or else he will tell everyone who I really am. Then I am surely to be tortured and murdered, and Hedy too."

"You don't know if that will occur."

"I do and so do you."

"You have seen his lab?"

"I have," Oskar said.

"Franz didn't just destroy Anna's gravesite like I told you. He took her body."

Oskar bowed his head. "I know."

"You know?"

"Yes, Father."

"Do you know where she is?"

"She is with me."

Mattheus straightened his back. "Explain."

Oskar stood. "It's better I show you. Come. Hedy can dress your injury once we are home."

Chapter Twenty

Inside their home, Hedy curtailed the bleeding and wrapped Mattheus' arm.

The priest explained, "I was on the roof, rolled off, and into a pile of hay. Thank God for the soft landing." He laughed with feigned jolly. "But when I stood, my arm was sliced. I realized I cut myself on a four-bladed hoe."

"That certainly was bad luck, Father," Hedy said.

"It could have been worse." He crossed himself.

Enduring cups of hot cider, Mattheus tried not to tighten his hands around Oskar's neck and scream, where is Anna, Finally, he said, "you were going to show me something?"

"Yes. This way."

"What?" Hedy asked her husband.

"I'm going to show him Anna."

"Should you?"

"It's okay." Oskar kissed her on the cheek.

Mattheus followed them to the studio behind the house. Inside, he surveyed the worktable and the steel and brick oven where a fire sparked and spat. The heat was so intense the priest felt it upon first entering the bungalow. He noted the annealer with its low orange and blue dancing flame, nearby jacks and the other handheld tools of a glassblower.

"There." Oskar pointed toward shelves lined with glass bottles.

Mattheus walked toward the rear of the shop. His arm throbbed but he was thankful Hedy had contained the bleeding. He peered into the containers. Some held ground particles, others corralled globs in liquid.

"Anna?" he dared to speak.

Oskar nodded.

"Franz did this?"

"Yes."

"What's in that glass jar?"

"Look closely," Oskar said.

Mattheus picked up the jar of yellowed stones and held it near his face. His stomach lurched as the realization overtook him. "Her teeth?"

"Yes," Hedy said.

Mattheus could barely speak, could hardly breath. "Is this all...Anna?"

"The Count commissioned me to make a memorial for her."

"A memorial for her, and *of* her." Hedy said.

"Out of glass?"

"Yes, Father."

"Can you do it?"

"I believe so."

"Will you?"

Oskar nodded.

"Desecrating a body is punishable by death. Report the Count to the authorities and your problems will be solved. Franz will be hanged by morning."

"He owns the guards, and he'll tell everyone about me and Hedy. Tribadism is also punishable by death although I am certain once everyone finds out the law won't have a chance to mete out our punishment."

"Then you must flee at once," Mattheus said.

"What about Anna?"

"Leave her with me. I will take care of her always." He picked up the jar containing her teeth and pressed it to his chest.

"No." Oskar took the container and placed it back on the shelf. "I want to make this memorial for her. I already have the plan. Four carousel horses made from Anna's remains mixed with sand and lime. The horses will sit on a revolving platform. Music will play when it rotates. I am certain it will work if I can get the formula right."

"If the Count shares your secret, you will have no opportunity to do this. That's why you must go at once."

"If I tell him he can do the surgery and then I delay it in time for me to make the horses..."

"Or," Hedy offered, "we can leave and take Anna with us, we can blow the horses elsewhere."

"I will have no oven, no annealer."

"I fear for you both." Mattheus picked up the glass jar again. "Go and I will let you know when it's safe to return."

"No, Father." Oskar took the container back from him again. "I came to you for your help. Running is not an option. This is our home. We have nowhere else to go. How shall we live, and in February no less when the weather is frigid?"

"Wolfgang will take us in," Hedy said.

Oskar placed Anna's teeth back on the shelf. "I'm not leaving without her."

"You are not leaving *with* her." Mattheus grabbed the jacks and held the metal tool in front of him. The heat from the flame of the brick oven lit the back of his frock.

"What are you doing?" Hedy asked.

"I'm taking Anna with me."

"I went to you because I trusted you," Oskar said. "You're supposed to help me."

"No one can help you. You're a freak. One of God's mistakes." He scooped up three jars with his injured arm and held the jacks in his other hand. "You're right. I never should have introduced the two of you but your families knew you were different and I thought freaks deserve to be together."

"Put those down," Oskar demanded.

"Please, Father." Hedy pleaded.

Mattheus looked from freak one to freak two, at the door across the studio, and then at the brick oven and its flame burning only steps behind him. He knew trying to escape with Anna was a terrible idea, impulsive, poorly thought out. With years of cutting and whipping weakening his body and his soul, he certainly was not agile enough to carry all of Anna back to the church, nor spry enough to outrun Oskar through the cold and snow. What would he do with her once he got her there anyway? He couldn't put her back together.

He placed the jars on the shelves and the jacks next to them. "Do you think she's the fortunate one?"

"What do you mean, Father?" Hedy asked.

"Perhaps she is in her better place. The Count can no longer withdraw her blood for experiments. He can no longer disrespect her by lying with others."

"What?" Oskar stepped toward him.

"He made her do horrible things. She would confess to me all the time."

"What things?" Oskar demanded.

"Experiments."

"She never told me."

"You have the evidence of his madness right here." He pointed to the jars. "Judgment day is here. And you, Oskar Glasman, are responsible."

"Me? How?"

"Why haven't you called the authorities to report what atrocities the Count has committed? Robbing her grave? Turning her into ashes? Why haven't you confronted the Count and struck him dead for his offenses?"

"Why haven't you? You were there when he took Anna's body. What have you done?"

"I am no ordinary man. What I witness goes straight to God who will hand out punishment in the afterlife. But here, as you are God's child on earth, it is the parishioner's responsibility to ensure order and to protect. Yet you do nothing but fire up your oven. You claim to be a man. You're not much of one, it seems. Didn't your parents teach you being a man is more than wearing the clothes and wishing you didn't have breasts? Didn't they instruct you it's not about being a man or a woman, but being human?"

"Do not speak to him like that," Hedy said.

Mattheus kept his eyes targeted on Oskar. "A real man would have protected the woman he loved."

"Anna and I were friends, the very best. I loved her, true. But how was I to protect her from what I did not know?"

"You were blind to her. You were only interested in your own needs."

"That's not true. Anna protected me. She didn't want me to know about Franz. She didn't want our friendship tainted by his lunacy. You are the sinner, Father. You knew how the Count treated her and you did nothing."

"He's right," Hedy said. "You're the one who was in love with her. You're the one who failed to protect her."

Dizziness overcame Mattheus and he swayed under the truth. The heat from the oven warmed his back. The not-yet-healed leather strap marks stung sweetly. He turned and looked at the fire. Flames have evoked images of hell since before Dante portrayed souls writhing and burning for all of eternity, but at that moment to Father Mattheus the conflagration was his version of heaven.

"Hedy is correct. I was in love with Anna and I failed to protect her." He turned back to Oskar and Hedy. A lightness about him now, a calm he had only experienced when with Anna. Not even God had made him feel this way.

Mattheus asked Oskar, "How is it that a man like Count Franz von Walsegg walks the earth when he has so mistreated Anna? How is he still able to enjoy the fruits of his riches and his excesses when he has threatened to expose you, endangering you and your wife if you don't allow him to mutilate your body. And for what? To satisfy his curiosity? For sexual pleasure? How is it you call yourself a man yet you have not yet stricken him dead?"

"Is that what makes a man?" Oskar asked.

"A man is made of different things at different times. What do you desire more, Oskar Glasman? Removal of your breasts so you can feel like a man while biologically still being a woman, or truly becoming a man by protecting the honor of the women you love?"

"Don't listen to him," Hedy said. "He is playing with your mind."

The priest edged toward the oven. "What real man listens to his wife over his priest? What real man obeys his wife over what he knows to be true in his heart? Your parents trusted me when they first brought Oskarina to Gloggnitz. I have not betrayed them. You must trust me now."

"Murdering Franz does not make Oskar a man."

Mattheus looked at Hedy. "And removing his breasts does?"

"No. I am not in favor of it. I love him for who he is, every part of him."

"It is not enough for you to love him, Hedwig. Oskar must love himself."

"Enough," Oskar said. "I am a man and I will make a decision that is best for me and best for my wife." He looked at the shelves. "And what is best for Anna in her honor."

"Good, my son. Now, one more thing before I go, do you know why Anna's last word before she died was to speak your name?"

"Perhaps," Hedy said, "she knew he would find a way to make her live forever."

"Then do the same for me." Mattheus threw himself into the oven.

Chapter Twenty-one

Oskar ran through the snow toward Stuppach Castle, leaving Hedy at the house. Their argument after overcoming the shock of Father Mattheus diving into the oven, of hearing his screams, of smelling his burning flesh, had been the worst ever. But Oskar knew Father Mattheus had been correct. Removing his breasts wouldn't alone make him a man. He needed to act like one. It was not enough to look like one on the outside. He had no intention to harm the Count, but he had had enough. It was time to put an end to the Count's control over his life. He would find a way to convince the Count to leave him and Hedy alone. He would handle this like a man and once the Count was no longer a threat, Oskar would go see Dr. Artz and have his breasts removed by a proper surgeon.

Oskar quickened his steps, seething the closer he got to the castle. The path to the front door came into view. On the doorstep, he rapped quickly. Manfred answered.

"I need to see the Count." Oskar stuck his hand into the pocket of his coat and felt the edge of the sharp tool. Just in case the Count wouldn't listen to reason...

"Is he expecting you?"

"I believe so."

Manfred bowed and closed the door. Oskar waited on the stoop under the grand entrance. His toes numb from the cold. Moments later, the door opened and Manfred led him in, past the library, and to the laboratory door.

"Forty-one steps down. Do you need a candle?"

Oskar rushed through the door and took the steps two at a time. Rage carried him into the darkness. At the bottom of the stairs, several candles flickered on a wooden table. The Count, dressed as a surgeon complete with a mask, was bent over the table. His hands adeptly held a tool that shimmered from the flames.

Oskar slowed his pace and cautiously made his way to the table. He hesitated to see what the Count was doing. His fears justified as the horrid smell hit his nose before the terrible sight met his eyes.

"Is that...?"

"Hello, Oskar. Have you come to accept my offer?" He did not look up.

"...an arm?"

Franz looped a last stitch through a post-mortem wound. "Just practicing. I'm not ready to perform your surgery at this moment, unless of course you'd like to do it without being anesthetized."

Oskar straightened his back, and again felt the knife in his pocket. He eyed the tools on the table next to the blackening arm. A surgical knife, a large needle, thread.

"Your offer is rejected."

Franz put the needle down. "I see. Well, that's kind of you to let me know in person. Perhaps you should wear a dress and makeup to Sunday's service."

"There won't be a Sunday service. Father Mattheus is dead."

The Count pulled the mask down around his neck. "Well, that is most unfortunate. I cannot say I liked the man. He showed too much attention to my wife. Fantasized about her, I'm sure, but he wasn't the only one."

"Anna and I were friends of the purest kind."

"Think what you like, Oskarina."

"My name is Oskar."

Franz grabbed the surgical knife and came around from behind the table. A few feet from Oskar, he said, "Your name is Oskarina and you are a woman. Accept who you are."

"My name is Oskar and I am a man. That is who I am."

The Count stepped closer. "You will never be a man with these." He placed a hand on his breast. "And this." Another hand plunged between Oskar's legs.

Oskar swatted his hands away and pulled the knife from his pocket. There would be no chance of reasoning with this monster. Why had he thought that possible?

Franz laughed. "What are you going to do? Your hand is shaking." The Count placed his knife on the operating table and circled Oskar. "I don't need a weapon because I know women don't have the same urges as men. They're not murderers. They're caregivers. You don't take lives. You give life. Maybe you should have a baby? Oh, wait, you and your wife don't have the right parts to make a baby. How is Hedy anyway?"

"Don't speak her name."

"How many times have I thought of fucking her? I think after everyone finds out about Oskarina, I'll bring Hedy back here and treat her as I have my lovely wife. What do you think of that?"

Oskar lunged the knife at him.

The Count jumped back. "Nice try but girls don't know how to fight. You should give me the knife before you get hurt."

Oskar lunged at him again. Franz hit his arm and knocked the knife to the floor. Oskar jumped onto Franz and wrapped his hands around his neck. The Count's knee to Oskar's stomach took his breath. Oskar rolled to his back. Franz jumped on him. Oskar fought back, arms and legs, kicking and striking. Franz punched him in the face. The blow sent Oskar's head reeling violently to the side. Another strike, blood seeped into his mouth. Franz restrained Oskar on the floor, his knees pinned his arms back. Oskar kicked his legs and tried to throw Franz off him but the Count was surprisingly strong. Franz pulled at Oskar's pants, tugged them down, Oskar's legs kicking and flailing, the Count frothing with psychosis. More blows to Oskar's face, to his stomach, and then Oskar felt the blade against his neck, not knowing where the knife came from and then realizing it was his own.

"You move again and I will kill you and then I will go to your home and dissect your wife."

Franz undid his pants.

Chapter Twenty-two

Blood dripped down Oskar's legs and carved a trail from Stuppach Castle to his home.

Hedy met him at the door and led him into the house. "My love, what happened to your face? Why are you walking so strange?"

"Franz will never bother us again."

She looked at the front of his pants, which were seeped in blood. "Are you cut?"

"He..." Oskar could not speak the words.

"Did he...?"

Oskar fell into Hedy, wept hard and long, gulped breaths as he sobbed and his body trembled. Hedy held him. They cried as one.

After several minutes, she steered him toward his chair in front of the wood-burning stove.

"Once they discover the Count's body, they will know it was me. Not only since I was the last to see him, but from my trail of blood from the castle to our home. I shouldn't have come here but I couldn't leave without seeing you, without telling you what happened."

"The snow, it's falling, it will cover your tracks."

"Yes, in time, I suppose."

"You were defending yourself. Surely they will believe that."

"How do I tell them what he did to me without revealing who I am?"

Hedy quietly said, "I do not know."

"To protect you, I must go."

"I am going with you."

"I'll send for you when I'm safe and settled. You must take care of something here first."

*

It was a day's journey by foot to Wolfgang's flat. Wolfgang would help Oskar find a haven and when the time was appropriate he would summon Hedy to join him. As Oskar made his way in the dark toward Vienna, he thought of Manfred's reaction when he had walked in on them and made just enough noise to distract Franz. Oskar sprung free. The knife, within reach. Oskar swung it wildly, felt it lodge somewhere. A low moan and a final breath.

"Go," Manfred ordered.

Oskar stumbled toward the staircase, up the steps, through the castle hallways, out the door, and into the cold.

Making his way toward Vienna, he shook from his mind any chance of not being held accountable for Franz's murder. He felt terrible leaving Hedy but knew her safety required his disappearance. One day, they would be reunited, and he would be whole.

He reached under his cloak, under his shirt, and released the binding around his chest. He let it fall until it was left behind like the skin of a snake, soon to be buried in the newly falling snow.

Chapter Twenty-three

Hedy tried to calm herself with a cup of hot cider but her hands shook. She put the steaming mug down and walked toward the back of the home. The shelves of the studio were lined with bottles and containers of Anna's remains. Father Mattheus had been turned to ash. The story cast about Gloggnitz was Count Franz von Walsegg had gallantly lost his life in a sword fight over Anna's honor. He was being revered as a hero. Shops and schools were closed. All were ordered to mourn his death for seven days and seven nights.

In the studio, Hedy fingered the tools of the glassblower. The flames in the oven burned bright. She poured bits of Anna into the oven and added what she believed to be the right mixture of sand and lime. She placed the pipe inside and gathered the gather. Over several days she worked to form four glass horses. She barely ate and drank and hardly slept. She concentrated thoroughly on her task and tried not to obsess if Oskar was okay. Wolfgang would get word to her of Oskar's safe arrival as soon as it was feasible.

After many trial runs, trying not to get frustrated when a horse looked like a mule or glass tumbled to the ground and shattered, she placed the last horse in the annealer to cool. With the heat from the annealer on her face, she peered in at the four stallions. A white Arabian. A yellow Palomino. A chocolate Bay. A spotted Appaloosa. She had used Anna's blood as well as plant dye for coloring and markings. Pieces of jewels that Anna had gifted to Hedy were used to decorate the saddles and reins. Anna's ashes and Father Mattheus's ashes, combined with sand and lime, made the horses. Good and evil, the holy and the unholy, the beautiful soul and the demented spirit.

It had been Oskar's intention to have the four horses on a platform that rotated and played music, just like the carousel he had seen as a child while with his parents. Hedy frowned. There weren't any parts of Anna left to make the glass platform. She contemplated her options, glad she had excelled as Oskar's assistant, ready to take the reins.

Chapter Twenty-four

James the groundskeeper cursed. He needed more dirt to cover Franz's grave within the Von Walsegg family crypt but the ground was too hard from the cold. He was still sore from when Franz had hit him while stealing Anna's body, but he had to return to work. He needed the money. Perhaps he had returned to work too soon. He tried to jam his shovel into the ground and wondered, where was Father Mattheus? He hadn't been seen in a couple of days.

James felt the satchel in his front pocket, the small silk bag he had found in Mattheus' room when the priest had failed to show up for a sermon. The stench had horrified the groundskeeper but he knew exactly what the shriveled thing was and who it belonged to. Having worked closely with Mattheus, he had seen the pastor's obsession with the Countess while she was alive and the deep, relentless morose he felt since her passing.

James again tried to stab the shovel into the ground and groaned, sure a few ribs had been broken by the Count. Bless the man who thrust a sword through the Count's heart. He didn't believe it had been a fight over the Countess's honor, more likely a fight over ale or a wager. The only thing that could make this moment better would be if he were burying Franz alive. He tried once again to loosen dirt from the hard, cold ground, without success.

Out of breath, he leaned on the handle of the shovel and

said, "Only someone with super human strength could get this done."

"James?"

He straightened. His hand gripped his side where pain stabbed.

"Are you okay?" Hedy asked.

James panted. "I don't know. My side is aching." He clutched his chest. "I think my heart is attacking."

Hedy went to his side and gently took the shovel from him. "It's too soon for you to be doing this. Why don't you go home and rest?"

"I have to finish burying the Count." He wheezed.

"I'll do it."

"You?"

"I'm stronger than I look."

"But a woman, no, I can't allow that. And it is too difficult to get dirt from the ground."

"No one will know. Go home."

A spasm shot up the right side of his body. He teetered and felt faint. "Are you sure?"

"I am positive. I will finish burying the Count."

"Leave him. I'll finish it tomorrow. He's half-buried any-way." James started to walk away then turned, awkwardly angling his upper torso to diminish his pain. "Have you seen Father Mattheus lately?"

"No. Maybe he went to visit family."

"I don't know of him having any family and he would have told me of his intent to travel. Anyway, say hi to Oskar. I heard he's out of town. Visiting relatives or something."

Hedy nodded, not speaking for fear her voice would betray her knowledge.

"Go home, James. Sit by the fire. Heal."

"Thank you, dear Hedy."

James limped away. When he was out of sight, and the dark of night covered her, Hedy dug up what dirt had been tossed on the Count's grave.

The End

About the Author

Joanne Lewis is a writer and attorney living in Fort Lauderdale, Florida. She is the author of award-winning mystery and historical novels and novellas.

Please visit Joanne's website: www.joannelewiswrites.com

Email Joanne at jtawnylewis@gmail.com

Please consider reading Joanne's other books.

The Forbidden Trilogy:

Forbidden Room, Book 1 of the Forbidden trilogy

Forbidden Night, Book 2 of the Forbidden trilogy

Forbidden Horses, Book 3 of the Forbidden trilogy

Michelangelo & Me Series:

Michelangelo & the Morgue (book 1 of 5),

Sleeping Cupid (book 2 of 5),

School of the World (book 3 of 5),

Space Between (book 4 of 5), and

Michelangelo & Me (book 5 of 5)

Stand Alones:

Bee King

The Lantern, a Renaissance mystery

Make Your Own Luck, a Remy Summer Woods mystery

Wicked Good, co-written with Amy Lewis Faircloth

I miss you, Pops.

Mama, I love you more.

www.ingramcontent.com/pod-product-compliance
Lightning Source LLC
Chambersburg PA
CBHW030552130626
46552CB00006B/2525

* 9 781939 181749 *